# THE FORGOTTEN AND THE FANTASTICAL 3

# Also by Teika Bellamy

**Editor:**

*Musings on Mothering* (Mother's Milk Books 2012)

*Letting Go* by Angela Topping (Mother's Milk Books 2013)

*Look at All the Women* by Cathy Bryant (Mother's Milk Books 2014)

*The Mother's Milk Books Writing Prize Anthology 2013: PARENTING* (Mother's Milk Books 2014)

*The Forgotten and the Fantastical* (Mother's Milk Books 2015)

*Hearth* by Sarah James and Angela Topping (Mother's Milk Books 2015)

*Oy Yew* by Ana Salote (Mother's Milk Books 2015)

*The Mother's Milk Books Writing Prize Anthology 2014: THE STORY OF US* (Mother's Milk Books 2015)

*Echolocation* by Becky Cherriman (Mother's Milk Books 2016)

*The Forgotten and the Fantastical 2* (Mother's Milk Books 2016)

*Maysun and the Wingfish* by Alison Lock (Mother's Milk Books 2016)

*Handfast* by Ruth Aylett and Beth McDonough (Mother's Milk Books 2016)

*Baby X* by Rebecca Ann Smith (Mother's Milk Books 2016)

*The Mother's Milk Books Writing Prize Anthology 2015: LOVE* (Mother's Milk Books 2016)

# THE FORGOTTEN AND THE FANTASTICAL 3

Modern fables and ancient tales

EDITED BY TEIKA BELLAMY

Mother's Milk Books

First published in Great Britain in 2017 by Mother's Milk Books

Front cover image 'Blodeuwedd' copyright © Georgie St Clair 2017
Cover design copyright © Teika Bellamy 2017
Introduction copyright © Teika Bellamy 2017
Illustrations copyright © Emma Howitt 2017

ISBN 978-0-9954516-4-3

Typeset in Georgia and Lt Oksana by Teika Bellamy.
Lt Oksana font designed by Lauren Thompson.
Printed and bound in Great Britain by The Russell Press, Nottingham,
on FSC paper and board sourced from sustainable forests.
www.russellpress.com

First published in 2017 by Mother's Milk Books
www.mothersmilkbooks.com

## SPECIAL THANKS TO:

My wonderful family who remain gracious and patient
with me while I run the press from home at all hours.
My co-editor and co-conspirator, Helen Lloyd,
who is a phenomenally fast and astute reader.
Emma Howitt and Georgie St Clair for being two of the most
imaginative and patient illustrators I've ever worked with.
The wonderful writers keeping fairy tales
alive and well in the world.
And all those who believe in me and Mother's Milk Books,
especially M.

# CONTENTS

# INTRODUCTION

*Fairy tales for breakfast,*
*fairy tales for lunch,*
*fairy tales gooey,*
*fairy tales with crunch.*

*Fairy tales at dinner,*
*fairy tales at night,*
*fairy tales fluffy,*
*fairy tales with bite.*

I read a lot of submissions for *The Forgotten and the Fantastical 3*, so much so, that I was aware that I was in danger of acquiring a jaded "literary palate". However, as always, there were stories that immediately took hold of my imagination and connected with me emotionally. These were, inevitably, the stories that made it into the anthology.

When I came to order the stories for the collection I realized that transformation was a key theme. The power of storytelling, as well as the potency of words and the imagination, was another theme. There were tragic endings and happy endings and endings in-between, as well as fascinating and inspiring female and male protagonists; in short, everything you could want from a modern collection of fairy tales for an adult audience.

So without further ado, let me introduce *The Forgotten and the Fantastical 3*. Enjoy!

**Teika Bellamy, Spring 2017**

# Silence Rose from the Water Like Steam

by

Poppy O'Neill

# Silence Rose from the Water like Steam

Every Sunday in the village beyond the hills the women would gather at the great lake to do the week's laundry. They did this work because they always had. On weekdays they dreamed and read and worked just as the men did, but each Sunday they walked together at dawn to the lake's edge carrying bags of washing.

They sang ancient songs as they dragged fabric through the water and beat it against the rocks. They hollered to the children if their games got too rough, muttering curses under their breath with a smile. The children ran and climbed and snaked through the trees.

One simmering hot day the women saw something flash and glide between them as their clothes floated through the water. Excitement spread as the creature became bolder, and the women gathered to watch its fast movements, its snout poking above the surface. One woman caught it easily with her quick, strong hands and held it aloft like a trophy. It hung quite calmly, as thick as a man's arm, dangling from her fist with just its forked tail flicking left and right. She put it in a wooden tub filled with clean water.

Everyone thronged around the tub to see the strange creature. It was long and limbless like an eel, but covered all over with iridescent fur. On its face was a beatific expression. It observed the women and children through its jewel-eyes, which could look in two directions quite independent of each other.

The children squealed and ran back to their games, shouting about the hairy eel, the sea monster, the Kraken. Now and then the smaller ones would return to their mother's breast for comfort and refreshment. One hand winding in her hair, one eye on the creature. The creature lay still and curled in the shallow tub, one eye on the children, one on the women.

After the initial wonderment had passed, the women continued with their work as before. They chatted and sang and whispered to and fro across the tub, now and then gently stroking the creature. It lay there, a perfect glittering spiral; silent and stoical.

But as their conversation passed back and forth over the tub, each word plopped into the still water and the creature, without moving, without changing its calm demeanour, consumed it. The names of all the women, their children and husbands, brothers, aunts and uncles. The names of their most intimate body parts, the words they used for the work they did. The names of fondly missed friends, the words they used to describe their lives. Their stories and the rhyme of their songs. Gentle soothing words, words of anger, words of memory. Each was lost to the water without even a ripple to show what had happened.

As the sun went down they fell into a contented silence. This was normal, as their arms and tongues became heavy from the day's toil. Silence rose from the water like steam and enveloped them.

It was only when they came to call their children back to the village that they noticed a change. The children's names were gone from the women's mouths. In each woman's mind she had the idea of her child, and she could see her image clearly, but when she opened her mouth no sound could bring that idea into the world.

Frightened and mute, the women climbed the rocks and trees to fetch their children back home. Every child was accounted for, but they walked with worry at the women's silence.

They approached the village as a crowd, arms linked in fear. The creature forgotten. The men frowned as the women tried to build meaning out of the small and useless words they had left.

For a week the women went about in near silence. Their minds saw and understood and had opinions on the world just as before, but their words had been wrung out of them. Problems went unsolved, ideas unrealised, jokes untold, worries unsoothed. Even written down, the words would not come. The women shrank inwards, trapped alone inside their own minds. They began to forget about each other: only those with voices can be heard.

*

The following Sunday they returned to the lake. The creature had been far from their thoughts so it surprised them to see it grown to many times its original size, curled still inside the wooden tub but now straining and splitting the sides. Its sleek fur shone and refracted the morning light.

The women did not need words for this, they knew what had to be done. Together they slid their hands under the creature's coiled body. It was bloated and sleepy but its snarl was loud and made of all the most precious words in their dialect. The women took the words back and began to sing, quietly at first. Holding firm, their strong calloused hands around its cold fur, they grew louder. They carried it, struggling and spitting their words back at them, to the lake's edge and with their combined strength plunged it in. As the water flew several feet into the air they raised their voices together in an ancient song, calling each other by name and changing the words as they pleased. The creature, now just a dark shape beneath the surface, slithered back to the depths of the lake. They continued the song for most of the day, as it had countless verses, each one endlessly adaptable. Call and response, improvised sections, actions when their hands were free. They were still singing as they walked, drunk on each other's company, back to the village.

# Midnight Riders

by

Dan Micklethwaite

# Midnight Riders

The cigar tip glows scarlet as Barry inhales. Smoke filters out of the side of his mouth and climbs like a beanstalk into the dark. It's a full moon tonight, though you wouldn't know it down here. There's only the fluorescent glare from the platform, lighting the flanks of the four white horses; they whinny conspiratorially amongst themselves, paw the earth, one of their hooves striking sparks off a rail. Their nervousness shivers through the loosely held reins.

He clamps the cigar between freshly veneered teeth, and frisks the pocket of his waistcoat for the gold-plated watch.

It's twenty to twelve.

They should be back soon. They know the rules, the curfew. When he dropped them off they were at their finest, their best possible selves. But fashion is time-sensitive. Beauty, too. Freedom.

Barry glances down mournfully at his well-contained paunch.

Winces at a twinge just behind his left knee.

He envied them earlier. The young men and young ladies, off out on the town. Their weekend's wish granted. Sitting here, lighting the first of (so far) four cigars, he waxed nostalgic, grew resentful. Part of him wanted to disregard the terms of his employment, the changed role he'd been roped into. Wanted to lock the door and stop them leaving. Let them slowly steam and gasp as the oxygen ran out.

But if he could call her now and try to negotiate a later time, he would.

After all, there's plenty yet to keep him going: a complimentary bottle of champagne in the footwell, a small picnic hamper still filled to bursting with a pre-midnight snack.

Alas, the business card she left – for emergencies only – is simply a sliver of platinum, with a slightly plump, bewinged silhouette stamped out through the centre, and nothing on the reverse. He fancies perhaps there's a special way to hold it in the moonlight, but down here he's at a loss. He puts it back in his pocket.

Even if there were a number, his phone's gone dead, and this carriage doesn't have any sockets to charge it; the only real problem with it that he's found.

Indeed, it was the thought of driving it again later that had cooled Barry's jealousy.

Driving is his life, in one form or another. Has been for going on twenty-five years. The accidents might have slowed him down, but they haven't stopped him. He's simply never found anything else he'd rather do.

In all of those years, no driving he'd done had ever felt better than this.

Not even in the stock cars he used to race, every third Sunday.

Not even the Ferrari experience a now-ex-wife had bought him, for a once-forgotten anniversary.

This, he thinks, is real horsepower. Their sleek white bodies still aglow in the platform lights. Still pawing, still nervous, but still elegant, too.

Though the one on the right at the back is a little portlier than the others, Barry feels a special affinity, a fondness for it. For *him*. She said their names earlier, but he only remembers this one's: Peachy.

Peachy seems to tremble more than the rest. Barry thinks it likely the horse is reluctant to relinquish this life for the old. He can relate.

He flips his watch out again. The second hand isn't slowing.

He ties the reins to the pommel and steps onto the platform. He stretches his legs, his left one especially. He throws his arms out and backwards, feels the fancy waistcoat, the girdle underneath it, tighten, and hopes the buttons don't pop. If the passengers do make it back in time then he still wants to be looking his best as well.

Wants the same for his carriage.

He stands and admires it; the gilded filigree patterns of climbing vines, the fruit in relief and ripe to bursting. He relaxes. He breathes smoke in a dense cloud that spirals daringly close to a fire alarm.

Then he tenses.

There is a spot, a smear of dirt, a splashback from the oily ground between the tracks, right there on the side of the ornately carved door. He removes the cigar from his mouth and then spits at the stain. He rolls up his jacket sleeve and wipes at it with his shirt, being careful not to scratch with his diamond-stud cufflink.

He steps back to inspect.

Satisfied, he limps away along the platform, along to the end of another branching corridor, which brings him to a deep buried concourse all silent and clean; no static through the station tannoy, and only a few stray pennies to recall the buskers who'd traded their stories during the day.

He stands at the foot of the escalators with the daunted awe of a novice climber. Their grated steps are speckless, their rails are burnished bronze. The white ceiling beyond could be mist, could be snow.

But no one descending them yet, and no hint that there will be.

He checks his watch.

Just about enough time to enjoy that champagne.

Peachy startles at the bang. The cork shoots out and away over his head into the darkness. Some of the fizz lands on Barry's hand and runs down to his wrist, where it finds the dirt on his cuff and bubbles it clear. There's no glass – another small oversight – but he's happy enough to swig straight from the bottle, remembering podiums, remembering wins.

Peachy's fear is contagious, though. A tremor hums throughout the ropey, sportive haunches of the other three steeds.

'Don't worry,' Barry says to them.

'This might last,' he says.

He checks his watch again. The big hand is so close that it's already touching the one, not nearly so far as he'd like from the two. In the distance, the far corridor, he thinks he hears voices. He stashes the bottle out of sight and steps onto the platform, tries to smooth down his outfit; to form a welcoming, deferential grin.

Remembers the cigar only when it singes his lip.

He takes one last, luxuriant drag, letting it go as the voices draw closer.

'Get ready, lads,' he says to the horses, 'they're going to make it. They're actually going to make it!'

Only, they aren't horses anymore.

Three lithe mice and a fat one loop in and amongst the maze of the harness.

Barry looks down at his drab blue blazer, his paunch, his scruffy brown suede boots.


The young men and young women return in a trickle over the next half hour. They file into the carriages in various states of undress and distress, in various degrees of coupling; some missing dignity, others just missing shoes.

One tall blonde in particular hobbles on board in a single

white stiletto, spins around the yellow pole accidentally, slumps into a seat. Barry waits for a suitor to stumble in after her, holding the other shoe, but none does. Mascara draws deltas down her sand-coloured cheeks.

Watching on CCTV in the cab, he recalls his ex-wives, them being dissatisfied, disappointed with his lack of real-world ambition; his self-destructive proclivity for the wrong kind of drive. The hospital stays, the scans, the limbs that competed with each other for most times held in traction. The repetitive, despairing messages scrawled in black marker on his casts.

Uncomfortable, he reaches inside his shirt, unfastens the clasps on the girdle, and slouches to the side, stretching his left leg as far as he can. This cab is too small, though. The dials too basic, too utilitarian. Even the monitor is low-res and glitchy.

He thinks of the business card and pats down his pockets. There's a part of this route where they'll be up at ground level, in the moonlight, the full moon, and it might just work then.

He already knows what he'll wish for: to travel this evening again from the top. To bypass the pettiness he'd felt at the start, and focus on providing a better service for his passengers. To get them there faster. Give them all another chance, he thinks, to make the most of what they have.

But he can't find the card anywhere.

And he won't, he realises.

It was in the other suit.


He looks away from the screen, through the glass, through the darkness. Up ahead in the tunnel, the signal goes green. He waits for the series of pneumatic *thunks*, the doors closing, each one like somebody swinging an axe. The engine revving up like the groan before *Timber!*

He sets his hand on the lever and the train eases forwards.

He can only hope that the mice have moved clear of the rails.

# The Web and the Wildwood

by

Lynden Wade

# The Web and the Wildwood

My Lord of Shalott is the kindest of husbands. He keeps me safe in this turret. In the room at the top, with guards at the door and the fast-flowing river all round the tower, we are both safe, he tells me, from the dark magic and the beasts and the robbers that dwell in the wildwood on the other side of the water.

He has rescued me from this wildwood, he says. I have no memory of it, so I must trust what he tells me. I am still under a curse, he says, but I will be safe from it if I am careful never to look out at the wildwoods. So that I have enough light, he's not bricked up the last window. A round mirror, large and slightly concave, in a carved wooden frame, has been placed opposite it. From anywhere in the room I can see the world. 'Just remember, my love,' he says, 'always look into the mirror, never out of the window. Or you will release the curse.'

I'm not lonely. My husband spends time with me every day, and comes to me every night. I have three ladies who attend to me: to my hair, my clothes, my food. I'm not imprisoned; I walk in the courtyard every day. I descend the spiral staircase, past the closed doors of the other rooms, and come into the light. The walls here are so high I can't see over.

I'm his most precious treasure, my husband says. He puts me in charge of his other treasures, bringing them up to my room for me to guard and cherish. I arrange them around me. On a stand I place the most beautiful book in the world, a Book of Hours with the capitals made out in gold and scarlet, with little grotesques down the margins. In a chest in the corner I pour the most gorgeous jewels in the world, red rubies and huge emeralds and strings of smooth, glowing pearls like moonlight rolled into balls. On a shelf on the wall I place the alchemist's jars, full of liquids and powders which, combined in the right way, can turn sand into gold. They clack when I push them up against each other, and the powder makes me sneeze until I have a headache.

I did have a pet rabbit to care for too, brought with me from the wildwoods when my husband rescued me. She had a wounded flank and I tended it carefully. Small and soft, with huge dark eyes, her powerful legs fought back at being picked up by anyone other than me. She lived in an airy cage by my bedside until one day, when I was walking in the courtyard, she squeezed her head between the bars over her head, and in her struggle to free herself, broke her neck. I wept, then howled, over her wrecked body, until my husband took me by the shoulders.

'That's enough, now. Rabbits are stupid creatures. I will buy you a monkey. They are far cleverer.'

He purchased my monkey at great expense. The merchant had brought him from a distant land they say is sticky with heat and fruit. My monkey is my delight, jumping from shelf to stand to bed, a moving treasure bounding round the collection.

But my lord still lacks one treasure. He longs for a unicorn's horn, to give healing powers to the muddy waters that swirl round this castle. The river is water for the peasants in the field, the monks that go riding to and from their abbey, the knights that gather in my lord's hall. With its healing powers, it could cure the ailing babies in the cottages, the old clerics with rheumy eyes, the knights with the sores on their legs from diseases picked up in the Holy Land. Because I love my husband I want to help him, but I cannot leave the castle. Instead, I'll advise him. And I will weave the story into my tapestry, for there's magic in the web, magic of my own making.

First I make a tapestry of the hunt. I weave a rampant lion, my lord's emblem, holding his shield and pennant. I weave the unicorn in the woods, dipping his horn in the animals' drinking pool so the water is safe and good for them all to drink. I weave a maiden sitting in the forest, waiting for the unicorn to be drawn to her purity. And I add my pet monkey, squatting beside her, because I love him.

Now we must try to recreate the scene. For the maiden I suggest one of my ladies, Aline, a knight's daughter. I stay safely in the tower and watch in the mirror as he and Aline leave with a small group of knights and ladies.

As he tells it, the unicorn was seen approaching at dusk; but just as it was about to lay its head on her lap my monkey leapt out of her skirts, chattering and shrieking, and the unicorn fled. Aline is confused. She says she had no idea that monkey was there, that he must have hid in the folds of her gown before she left the castle. My husband accepts this with a sigh, and hands my pet back to me. My tapestry is just a pretty picture.

We must lure the unicorn another way. We will offer it a garland of roses with the sweetest smell. It will draw near and then the one who holds the garland will step back – and back – until the unicorn is surrounded by the knights. I weave a new tapestry. I'm there, making a delicate garland. I weave in Monkey, smelling a rose. We choose the little kitchen wench to hold the garland. My husband insists that she wash well first, to get rid of the kitchen grease and the smell of onions.

The tapestry turns out to be a lie. As the kitchen girl is holding the garland out, my monkey jumps out of a bush, snatches the garland and runs away with it.

'You must not weave the monkey into the tapestry,' says my husband. 'He is stopping the capture of the unicorn.' He's brought my monkey home in a cage, but he unlocks it to return my pet to me.

I think long and hard about the third attempt. The answer

comes to me that evening, when the wind is up, sucking round the turret, and my husband asks me to play to him on the organ. It is a fine instrument, portable, with ivory keys; he had it made just for me, measured carefully so it would fit through the door of the turret. The next morning I begin a new tapestry. In it Aline and I play wonderful music on the organ. Around us I weave all the animals of the forest, drawn to the sound – the wolf, the ferret, the owl – and my little monkey. To hide my rebellion I weave him hidden behind a tree in the distance, just a paw, a cheek and an eye showing.

The organ was quite a trial to get out into the wildwood, I'm told; it kept sliding about in the cart. And Aline forgot her fingering at times as she played. I think that's what stopped the unicorn from coming. Only a glimpse of white flank was spotted in the undergrowth, but the men swear they heard the chattering of my monkey. When the little creature is found again, hiding in a tree at the edge of the forest, my husband has him brought home and chained to a log.

'Enough of women's ways,' says my husband. 'I will hunt the unicorn with hounds.'

So he goes hunting. I watch him in my mirror as he leaves, with horses and dogs. He is away all day. I am bored without him, and I start on another tapestry. I don't need to please him with this one, so I please myself.

This time, as my shuttle goes in and out, I am amazed with the precision of the thousand flowers I'm weaving into the tapestry. How do I know how to shape the petals and leaves? I can see them in my mind's eye. I can smell the sweet scent of the briar; hear the welcoming whisper of the oak leaves; feel the pleasing roughness of the bark. In my mirror I can see trees and rushes on the riverbank, but distance blurs the details. My knowledge comes from some other source. The animals, too, are picked out in wonderful detail; little rabbits with perked ears, a fox with his clever snout, a stoat with his lissom body, a bristly boar.

I stand back and look at the scene. My hands have chosen to weave a wood full of beauty, not menace. The stoat's claws are sharp, the boar's tusks powerful, but they hold no terror for me.

What's harder is people. So far, I have only woven myself and my ladies; now I want to portray some men in the hunt. I search the depths of the bowl-like mirror for inspiration. In the far distance some countrymen lean over their scythes. Along the road a pony plods with an abbot on its back. Two of my lord's household, who were delayed by attending a sick horse, appear in reflection as they hurry to join the hunt. Then there's a flash in the mirror. Something dazzling is passing by. I flinch back from the glare and find myself looking out of the window in search of its source.

It is a knight on horseback, on the road that skirts the castle. Not one from Shalott: his shield bears the emblem of the Grail. I can just see his face from here, under his plumed helmet. He wears a brown beard. It's Sir Lancelot.

How do I know that? I have never met that famous knight, have I? I've just heard of him from my ladies, who chatter about his latest deeds. I only remember what they told me: that he bears the symbol of the quest he never quite achieved.

I turn back to the room and pick up the shuttle again, but memory is scrabbling at my mind, like my monkey when he wants me to pet him. Lancelot without a helmet. Sitting, talking. Talking with my husband. Rising when I come in, bending over my hand. Why have I forgotten that? I stand quite still, willing the memory back. It clears, like a rippled pool returning to calm. Now I remember the room. Not my own: it has a banner over the fireplace, with the same Grail emblem. Sir Lancelot's own castle, maybe.

I turn back to the window. The road has taken a bend to the right and Sir Lancelot is out of sight. But now another memory has come. My husband and Lancelot under a window – not this one, I don't think, a lower one and wider, with a different view. Lancelot is arguing with my husband.

'Let her go, my friend. Wood sprites are born to live in the trees and the streams. No good ever comes of capturing a fairy bride.'

'Nonsense! The best houses are descended from fairies. As soon as I get her back to my castle she will forget where she comes from and be contented as a mortal woman.'

'*You* won't be content. She'll wilt away, slowly but surely. You think you'll hold her forever, but what you'll have won't be what you wanted.'

'Listen to you! On your eternal quest for the Grail, saying you'll be content when you've found it.'

'To see it. Not to hold it. That's the difference.'

I look away across the fields at the peasants. They are taking a rest, rubbing their backs and talking: their faces are ugly with toil and resentment. The abbot is coming back to the abbey: he is flabby with fat and greed. The household knights are still to be seen walking towards the forest: they are bragging to each other and bridling at each other's taunts.

I turn back to look around the room I've been in ever since my husband took me from the woods. I run my hand along the edge of the book's cover and see that it's singed from the raid in which it was captured. I pick up a rope of jewels and look closely at it; I find little flakes of old blood, almost black, caught in the setting of the emerald. I scan the alchemist's set and notice that the lotions are drying up and the powders all gone. Next to it sits the collar my little rabbit once wore.

I'm as stupid as she was. My lord won't let the unicorn go after it's purified the water. He'll keep it in the castle, away from its home. I must rescue it.

'I'm going to walk in the courtyard,' I say to the guards outside my door.

They do not argue with me. I've always been allowed to walk when it suits me; my husband trusted my fear of being cursed if I looked any further than the boundaries of the castle. Now I know what the curse is, and it has come upon me. It is to see the world as it really is.

There are huge bolts on the inside of the gate in the courtyard, and I need to stand on tiptoe to reach the top one, and tug and twist. It is heavy to open and creaks a protest. Outside are two steps down from it to the water; a little boat bobs there. A cool breeze drifts over the river and caresses my cheek. It brings with it the scent of pine from the farther shore – from the wildwood. I carefully untie the boat. I am still holding the rope when I hear the braying of horns, the barking of dogs and the shouting of men. Out of the wood on the edge of the shore bursts a small white beast that leaps into the water and begins to swim frantically. It is about the size of a goat, with a little white beard. It is far smaller than the one I wove, but it bears a long sharp horn on its forehead. I push my boat out but I keep hold of the rope. The little unicorn hooks its hoofs over the edge of the vessel and I pull him into the boat.

It is then that the hunt breaks out of the wildwoods. At the front the men drive a horse and over its back is slung the unicorn from the tapestries I wove before today. It is just as I depicted it; strong and fierce and pure and beautiful. The little one is its foal, maybe. Blood trickles from my unicorn's mouth. Its eyes are glazed over. It is quite dead. This is worse than I feared. It's too late for the mother, but I can save the foal. The little unicorn leaps after me as I leave the boat and return to my tower. We scramble up the stairs and when I am back in my room I grasp the shuttle in my hand. Deftly, I weave myself and the little unicorn into my tapestry. We will be safe here –

safe from the real dangers, not the ones my husband used in his efforts to keep me. And we will be free.

At the last minute my little monkey jumps in and joins us.

# Listening to the Mermaidens

by

Angi Holden

# Listening to the Mermaidens

I was seven the first time. I'd had a row with me mam, and she'd sent me to my room. I packed a few things in a duffel bag; it was time to leave home. I slipped out the back door, and down the lane towards the coastal path that skirted the village. A sea breeze buffeted the spiky clumps of gorse clustered along the verges. I was crossing the ridge when I heard a woman singing and I crawled to the cliff edge to peer over. There she was, sitting on a rock, salt spray freckling her body, her long blonde hair sweeping down her back. Oh, so beautiful. And in her arms was a tiny baby with curly black hair, held close to her breast. She didn't try to hide the baby, like my auntie when she fed our cousin; she just nursed her baby and sang to it.

I must have gasped, because she stopped singing and turned to look at me. For a moment she seemed afraid. She slipped from the rocks, still clasping the baby, and I cried out as she dipped below the water. I expected to see her surface again, but she was gone, even though I waited until the moon disappeared behind the clouds.

I tried to tell mam, but she was only interested in hugging me. I wasn't to make up stories, she said. She wasn't cross with me, but she'd been worried, and I wasn't to go packing my bags again. I didn't. I wanted to stay close to the cliffs, where I could watch for the woman on the rocks.

I was twenty-one when I saw another. I say 'another' because as soon as I saw her I knew she wasn't the same woman. This woman was darker, and smaller, with broad hips and a slender waist. But her voice was the same, clear and high-pitched, and the song was the same one that drew me to the cliff edge when I was a boy.

I'd more sense than to tell my mam this time. And I'd certainly got more sense than to tell my mates. It was my secret, and I kept it well. So well, that even the woman didn't know that every night I watched her clamber out of the sea to perch on the rock with her child. It was only when the baby spotted me and waved that she realised. I never saw her again.

There have been others over the years. Sometimes more than one – two or even three – so that there was hardly room for them to settle on the rock with their babies. Their voices twisted in the sea breeze, tangling like seaweed and then separating as if the wash of the tide had teased them apart. And I lay still on the cliff top, watching and listening.

I was seventy before I told anyone again. She was a carer at the convalescent home they put me in that winter, after I slipped and broke my hip. They'd put me on some strong painkillers; the manager said I'd gone a bit delirious. A bit funny in the head. But the girl believed me, the one who came with the tea in one of those sippy beakers, the ones that make you feel like a kiddie. Here, she'd say to me as she put the beaker to my lips. You sup this and I'll sing to you. I heard the song, and I knew. And she knew I knew.

And she smiled.

# Melissa's Bearskin

by

Ronne Randall

# Melissa's Bearskin

When Melissa was thirteen years old, she found a bearskin.

It was lying on the forest floor, right in front of her, so she picked it up. It was heavier than she expected. Heavy – but very, very soft. The fur was thick, silky, rich chestnut-brown, and when she held it to her cheek, the long hairs tickled and made her feel shivery in a strange and exciting way. The underside was soft, too, and smooth as a peach.

In truth, she did not know it was a bearskin – she only knew that it was a beautiful furry thing, and that holding it close made her happy. So, because it was a cold November day and she had only a thin knitted cloak over her dress, Melissa wrapped the fur around her shoulders and ran home to show her mother.

Melissa's mother, Lilasette, was a Wise Woman. She knew the ways of the forest, and she knew how to heal people and animals with plants and herbs. She had been taught by her own mother, Melissa's grandmother Rose, and now she was teaching Melissa. But Melissa was flighty and impatient and didn't always listen.

What Melissa did want to know more about her mother's past. Her mother, she knew, was the daughter of a prince and had once lived in a palace.

'Does that mean I am a princess too, Mother?' Melissa once asked her.

'I wish better things for you, my precious child,' Lilasette answered.

'But what could be better than being a princess?' Melissa wanted to know.

'Living a life of truth and kindness and harmony with all living things,' Lilasette replied.

Melissa thought for a moment or two.

'I think I would rather be a princess,' she said.

Now, when Melissa showed her mother the treasure she had found, Lilasette's brow furrowed and her eyes clouded with concern.

'This is a bearskin,' she told Melissa, running her hand over the velvety skin. 'It belongs to someone, my darling, and they will be missing it. You must put it back where you found it.'

Melissa snatched it back from her mother. 'No!' she said. 'I found it, so it's mine. I love it, and I'm keeping it. It makes me feel like... like a princess!'

Lilasette sighed and shook her head. Much as she loved her daughter, she sometimes felt powerless in the face of her wilful obstinacy.

'It is better to be a good and generous person than the most privileged princess, my daughter,' she said. 'The owner of this bearskin might come to harm without it. How would you feel, knowing your actions caused someone unhappiness or pain?'

Melissa turned away. She didn't want to hear the truth in her mother's words.

'All right,' she said at last, heaving a resigned sigh. Taking the beautiful fur from her mother, she left the cottage, her eyes downcast.

But Melissa did not take the bearskin back. She told herself that she couldn't remember where she had found it, and she made herself believe her own lie.

Instead, Melissa found an old hollow log. She carefully rolled up the bearskin and put it inside, safe from her mother's eyes.

Neither Melissa nor Lilasette spoke of the bearskin again. But Melissa made sure it stayed safe inside its hiding place. She visited it almost every day, when she went walking in the forest, and when she went out to gather healing plants for her mother. Sometimes she took it out and wore it for a while, just to feel the silky fur against her skin. She would pretend that she was a princess dressed in a cloak of ermine. But in her heart she knew that no ermine cloak would ever be as soft and luxuriant, as comforting and gentle, as her precious bearskin.

And so two years passed this way. Melissa grew taller and more rounded in her hips and bosom. Still the bearskin wrapped and covered her perfectly, and its fur still embraced her with warmth and tenderness.

One morning, a woman from the village brought her baby to Lilasette. The baby was red and hot with fever. While Lilasette gently bathed him, she sent Melissa out to gather rosemary and elderflower so she could make the baby a soothing, cooling potion.

Her basket swinging on her arm, Melissa walked along the familiar forest path, singing as she went.

*Tell me who I'll marry,*
*Tell me who he'll be,*
*While the river gently flows*
*By the greenwood tree...*

'That's a lovely song,' a deep voice said. 'And you sing it so beautifully. Your voice is as sweet and smooth as honey.'

Melissa stopped short. A tall young man emerged from behind a broad oak tree and walked towards her. He had deep brown eyes and chestnut-coloured hair – hair that looked as soft and silky as her bearskin. Melissa's heart leapt into her throat, and her knees wobbled.

'Who are you?' she whispered.

'My name is Berendt,' said the young man. 'Who are you?'

Melissa told him her name, and explained why she was in the forest.

'I have to hurry home to help my mother,' she said, 'but perhaps we could meet here tomorrow?'

'Yes,' said Berendt. 'I would like that. I would like to know more about you, Melissa with the honey voice.'

And so, the very next day, Melissa went to the broad oak tree. And there was Berendt. They sat together and talked, and soon Berendt took Melissa's hand. His own hand was smooth and warm, like silken leather. Melissa held it tight.

Melissa and Berendt met every day after that, and the love they had both felt that first day grew and blossomed and bore fruit. Ten weeks after they first met, Melissa's courses failed to come. Then she started throwing up her breakfast.

Lilasette noticed, but said nothing. And Melissa said nothing to her. But she told Berendt.

Berendt threw his arms around her and pressed her to his chest. 'I love you, Melissa, and I love our baby who is growing inside you,' he said. 'But I have a secret I must tell you. I should have told you sooner – now you have to know.'

'Are you a prince?' Melissa asked. 'You are as handsome as a prince!'

'No,' said Berendt, unclasping his arms. Melissa was astonished to see tears in his eyes and pain twisting his face. 'But you are right in one way. I am not what you think I am.'

'Are you a criminal hiding from the sheriff?' Melissa asked, her voice trembling. 'Or do you have a wife and babies already?'

'No, my only love, my only heart,' said Berendt. 'It is worse than either of those.'

Melissa's blood froze. 'What could be worse?' she whispered.

'I am not a man,' said Berendt.

'What do you mean?' Melissa asked. 'Of course you are a man! I know you are young – we both are – but you are more than a boy. Your manly arms have held me close. You have planted your seed in my body, and we have made a child together, a child whose heart is now beating within my womb. Only a man could have done that.'

Berendt looked away, and his tears flowed freely now.

'I am not a man, nor even a boy,' he said. 'I am not human. I am... a bear.'

Melissa felt every part of her begin to quake. Her tongue stuck in her mouth, and her throat closed so she could not speak. Berendt took her hand again, and this time, when she felt the soft, silken leatheriness of his palm, she knew he was telling the truth.

'I am a bear,' he repeated, 'and my home is a den deep, deep in this forest. One day, I stole a honeycomb from a hive and angered the Queen Bee – and she put a spell on me. Her workers took away my bearskin and turned me into a man. The spell was only supposed to last for a day and a night – she was going to give me my skin back. But the worker bees dropped my skin, and someone took it, and now I must remain a man forever.'

Melissa felt as if the broad oak tree above them was pressing on her chest.

'Is that so bad?' she asked Berendt. 'Can you not remain a man? We could be married. We have a child coming. Could you not be happy with that?'

'Melissa,' said Berendt, taking her in his arms once again, 'I am a bear. I will always be a bear, even if I have human skin. And I can never be whole or happy without my bearskin. I search for it every day, and I will search forever until I find it and once more become who I am.'

His eyes were full of pain, and Melissa's were full of tears. Her mother's words echoed within her, keeping time with her pounding heart: 'The owner of this bearskin might come to harm without it...' She loved Berendt more than anyone on earth and would do anything to make him happy. But if she returned his bearskin, she might lose him forever.

'Oh, my love, my love, my only love,' she wept, soaking his tunic with her tears.

That night Melissa slept fitfully. Though she had never been near an ocean, she dreamed of being in a small boat, thrashing about on a wild and stormy sea. As she was cast into the waves, Berendt rose up from beneath the churning water and caught her in his arms.

'You saved me!' she cried, as he held her and swam towards shore.

'Yes,' he said, 'as you would save me if you could. As you would save me...'

When she woke, Melissa knew what she had to do. Though she felt that she was walking to her doom, she made her way to the broad oak tree.

Berendt was waiting for her as usual, his eyes darker and sadder than ever.

'My love,' she said, taking his hand, 'I will help you find your bearskin.' Then, slowly, with her heart shattering into smaller pieces at every step, she led him to her hollow log.

'Look inside,' she said.

Berendt withdrew the bearskin and held it up with a cry that contained both anguish and joy. He flung his arms around Melissa and whispered, 'Human or bear, I will love you always, with all my heart and with all my might.'

'Human or bear, I will love you too, Berendt,' Melissa whispered back.

Berendt started to say something, but his voice caught in his throat.

'What is it, my love?' asked Melissa.

'You could come with me,' said Berendt. 'Come and live

with me in my forest den, and we will raise our child together.'

Melissa bowed her head. 'It cannot be,' she whispered. 'I will always be human. You will always be bear. Our worlds are not the same.'

Berendt knew she was right.

'Keep our child safe within you, and when he is born, bring him to me so that he may know who his father is,' said Berendt. 'You will know where to find me.'

Then he put on the bearskin – and, with a shudder and a glow in the air around him, he vanished. An instant later, standing before Melissa was a strong, handsome bear with chestnut fur and deep brown eyes. Those eyes locked with Melissa's, and a soft grunt emerged from the bear's throat.

Melissa ran to him and embraced his large, hairy body as best she could, burying her face in his silken fur. She was saying goodbye to her beloved Berendt, and to the bearskin that had brought her such pleasure, and she wept with every fibre of her being.

Then she ran home, not looking back.

Melissa told her mother everything. Lilasette held her daughter and comforted her and assured her that when it was time for her baby to be born, she would be there to help ease its entrance into the world.

'And if you have a daughter,' Lilasette said, 'she will learn to be a Wise Woman, just as you are becoming.'


As Melissa's belly and breasts swelled over the next months, Lilasette nourished her and her growing child with warming soups and calming tea brewed from gentle herbs.

Then one night, when the full moon glowed orange in the sky, Melissa's womb began to contract and her waters broke. She laboured with all her might, and cried out lustily as she pushed her baby – Berendt's baby – into the world.

Melissa did not hear her mother's gasp as she delivered her child, but when she heard the baby's cry that was not a cry but a howl, her heart trembled and ached and she bellowed with joy and grief and fear.

Lilasette tried to take the baby away, but Melissa's arms and breasts and soul ached for him. 'Give him to me,' she sobbed. 'Please, Mother, give him to me.'

And she put the tiny baby, covered with downy brown fur, to her breast. His leathery paws were soft against her skin, pushing with gentle pressure as he suckled. And so they lay together in the moonlight, until they both fell asleep.

The next day, Lilasette helped Melissa wrap the baby in a soft woollen shawl. At the last moment, Melissa took the red velvet ribbon that held her long golden hair, and put it inside the blanket – so that her son would have something of his mother's to hold. Then she set out, clutching her child to her breast.

When she came to the broad oak tree, Berendt was there. He reared up on his hind legs and uttered a cry when he saw Melissa – a cry that contained both joy and anguish. With him was a she-bear, a cub clinging to her back. Melissa could see that the she-bear's breasts were heavy with milk, so she knew her child would be nourished – with food, if not with the mother's love that only she could give him.

Melissa wept as she returned home. And though it was springtime and the air was warm, she began to shiver, with a coldness that rose from deep within her. When she got home, Lilasette lit a fire and brewed a tea of ginger and cinnamon, sweetened with honey – but nothing was enough to warm Melissa.

'My bearskin would keep me warm,' she wept. 'I need my bearskin.'

\*

Moons waxed and waned, and winters and summers came and went. At first Melissa thought the aching, broken place inside her would never be whole again. But slowly, as the seasons passed, Melissa's fractured heart began to knit itself back together. In time she met a young woodsman named Lionel, and his kind eyes and gentle ways won her affections. He built a small cabin for them near Lilasette's cottage, with a great stone oven big enough to heat a house three times its size. He hoped it would keep his beloved Melissa warm. She was always cold, it seemed.

One day, when Lionel returned from his work in the forest, he shouted for Melissa.

'I have a surprise for you!' he said. She rushed out – a bit clumsily, as her belly was big with their first child.

'I was chopping wood,' said Lionel, 'when suddenly a bear came out of a thicket and ran towards me. It was terrifying, but I managed to kill him with my axe. And look! I have brought this home for you. It is so silky, so soft – surely this will keep you warm!'

He held out a bearskin – silky, thick, chestnut brown fur. And tangled up within it – a red velvet ribbon.

# The Narclops

by

Sophie Sellars

# The Narclops

'Tell me the story of the Old World, Grandpa,' she says, settling down in her bunk.

'Why would you want to hear of such things before bed? You won't sleep!'

'Do you remember it? The mountains and the forests, the deserts and the seas –'

'The seas! I certainly remember the seas; hard to forget the seas,' he says, as he sits on the edge of her bed, the thrash of waves as clear in his mind as the day of the Flood. 'I don't want to give you nightmares.'

'You won't!' she says. She has heard the stories before, knows all about the monsters. They're not like the monsters in the other tales. They have no sharp teeth or claws. They don't even frighten her, not in that way. But they linger in her mind and wrap around her thoughts, puzzling her with the mystery of their two eyes that became one.

'Well, just for a moment. But don't tell your mother,' he whispers. 'She doesn't like me filling your head with these stories, especially before bed.'

Her face glows with the pleasure of a secret shared.

'Long ago, before you came to be, when I was just a small boy myself, we lived in the Old World. It was a magnificent place with towering mountains, lush forests, vast oceans and great frozen caps of ice. It was home to a multitude of species; some survived, some disappeared, but eventually, the humans came to dominate. There were far too many of them. Half of them were extremely poor, desperate for food and water and prone to sickness and disease. The other half were extremely rich, with more food than they could eat and a voracious appetite for frippery.'

'What's frippery, Grandpa?'

'Things. Stuff. Unnecessary bits.'

She looks at him blankly but he is mid-flow, like the floods that eventually claimed the Old World, and she knows better than to interrupt him.

'The irony was that the people who had everything wanted more, and they plundered the earth, destroyed the forests and poisoned the seas in their greediness.'

'Were you alive during this time, Grandpa?' she asks.

'I was, but it was very near the end at that point. Much had changed in a hundred years. First the computers came, which helped simplify the work of the people, but then the Net arrived, which altered everything. The Net was all-powerful, it couldn't be seen and it couldn't be touched, yet it held all the answers and the people were entranced by it.'

Whenever she heard mention of the Net, she always pictured one of their fishing nets being hauled up from the lake, a shoal of humans caught inside it, their wet faces pressed against the mesh; eyes wide, mouths agape. She always felt sorry for them.

'Gradually, the humans began to turn away from the towering mountains and from what remained of the lush forests; they ignored the cry of the oceans and the scream of the ice caps, so enthralled were they by the information at their fingertips.'

'But information is a good thing!' she says, frowning.

'It is a good thing, you're right. But so much of the information available was meaningless. You see, the humans left their waste wherever they went, and the Net was no different. The amount of junk caught up in the Net exceeded the amount they threw into their seas, and one of the most toxic things it ensnared was the Book.'

'But books are good things!'

'Books are excellent things, but not this book. It was a book of faces, their faces, and its arrival heralded the end of exploration, for once the Book came to be, people stopped looking outwards and only looked at themselves.'

'So, the Book was written by the humans?'

'Of course, although it charmed them like the word of God. And by the end, its importance exceeded that of their bible.'

She ponders this for a moment. 'The bible – was that the one about the man who could walk on water? Who made lots of sandwiches?'

He hesitates before nodding. She's in the right ballpark.

'What was written in the Book, Grandpa?'

'Anyone could choose to read the Book and have their own page inside it. A page all about themselves, their news, their thoughts, information on what they were doing, photographs of themselves. Their cats.'

Cats. She was pretty sure she'd learned about those in Earth Sciences; self-powered motor vehicles that were widely used by humans for transportation. A bit like the levipods they had here, only terrestrial.

'Was it an interesting book, Grandpa?'

'They certainly thought so and their obsession with it consumed them, to the point where their need to have things was no longer enough. They needed to *show* people that they had things.'

She scowls as she tries to make sense of this.

'You see, despite the towering mountains, lush forests, vast oceans and great frozen caps of ice, the thing humans liked to look at the most was themselves, and the Book was like an enormous mirror. But they also wanted everyone else to look at them, so everyone clamoured for everyone else's attention by adding more information about themselves to the Book, adding more photographs, sharing more of their thoughts.'

'But sharing is good!' she reasons.

'You're right! Sharing is good. It usually implies compassion and kindness.'

'A bit like that man with the sandwiches again, when he fed the hungry.'

'Exactly! But you see it wasn't that sort of sharing. The poor half of humans were still starving, still desperate, still struggling for survival.'

'And the rich half didn't help them?'

'Some tried, attempts were made, but help like that was seen as an act of charity by a mere few rather than a collective instinct as we have here. Most people would look and remark how terrible it was, before turning back to their reflections in the Book. The only thing they were readily inclined to share was information about themselves.'

It all seems so odd to her, so alien to the principles of her world where *There Is No Self* was a hymn that hummed at the heart of their society, and altruism was as instinctive as breathing.

'So, what happened next?'

'Well, the Book wasn't the only means to perpetuate a self-enhancing fiction; there were other traps hidden in the Net. One was like a hall of mirrors with only pictures, I forget its name, and there was another one, some kind of aviary where humans would squawk at each other like birds.'

She explodes into giggles, stuffing her face into her pillow so as not to wake her brother next door.

'What on earth were they thinking?'

Her grandfather smiles at her sadly.

'It's easy to laugh at them now, but there's a poetry to it, a kind of poignancy; the desperate need to be noticed, to etch some small mark in the wasting sediment of their mortality. And you forget, had they not made the mistakes that they did as individuals, our species would not have progressed to embody the collective consciousness that we have now.'

She wipes her eyes, suppressing her giggles so that her grandfather will continue.

'Anyway, where were we? Oh yes, the Flood.'

She pulls her bed covers up to her face, her mood sobering. 'While all this self-worship had been going on in the Net, the humans failed to notice the damage being wrought on their world. Evil had prospered while they'd been looking the other way. Those were bad times, troubled times –'

Her grandfather sighs, his shoulders slumping as he recalls the tyrants that came to power and the poisons they unleashed. Truths too brutal for bedtime.

'The humans had yoked themselves to the small device that fed their vanity, always hunched over it, continually voicing their wisdoms and immortalising themselves in self-portraiture, unaware that they were losing the ability to see anything outside of the Net.'

'Did they never look up?'

'Hardly ever. I remember when my father took us to the ancient pyramids of Egypt. This was your great-grandfather, of course, one of the Pilgrims. He was a well-travelled man and was keen to instil in us the same love of exploration, the same appreciation of the physical world that he had. He shunned the Book and only used the Net as was absolutely necessary for his work; he was very unusual for his generation.

'He had long wanted to visit Egypt, to see the mysteries of this ancient land, and I'll never forget how his face fell as we drew up in the dusty surrounds of Giza; his smile fading like the timeworn contours of the Sphinx. For in front of us was a crowd of people who, like us, had travelled far to visit the pyramids of Egypt, yet they had turned away from this ancient marvel and were standing with their backs to it, their devices outstretched to capture themselves.'

Her mouth falls open in astonishment.

'One of the Seven Wonders of the Old World reduced to a mere backdrop,' he continues, 'a pilgrimage taken for the sake of a status update.'

She shakes her head.

'Eventually, man was subsumed entirely by his digital counterpart. With each self-portrait, each update, each cry for attention, his soul had ebbed away until there was nothing left. Blinded to the physical world around him, he had surrendered to the single eye of his device, and on its screen, he saw only himself. Cyclops had joined with Narcissus, and the monster was born.'

'The Narclops,' she whispers, the tragic fate of which had been discussed for as long as she could remember.

'A wretched beast: a victim of its own vanity, a slave to its own ego. Technology had seized the empty shell of humanity, who had given themselves willingly. Shortly afterwards, the ice caps of the Old World melted and the devastation was more than anyone could have possibly imagined. The floods came and life on Earth was wiped out. The Narclops peered over the brink, staring at their own reflections in the water until it consumed them.'

For a moment, she is silent, too submerged in the story to speak. And then she remembers something.

'But my great-grandfather and the rest of the Pilgrims, they managed to escape.'

'Yes, what they did was very brave, very dangerous... and very naughty.'

'Naughty?'

'Well certainly! You've heard of their rebellion. How their routine voyage to Mars was halted once the flooding began, but they launched their craft anyway, bundling their families into its cargo bay at nightfall and propelling themselves out into the galaxy just as the last waves devoured the Earth. And the excruciating peril of that first wormhole and the strange destiny that flung us out of it towards –'

He looks at his granddaughter. She is sitting upright, her eyes wide, her small fists gripping the bedclothes as she hangs onto every word.

'But those are stories for another night; you need to get some sleep!'

'But Grandpa!' she whines.

'No buts! Goodness me, you've kept me here much longer than I meant to be.' He gets up from her bed, straightening the cover over her. 'I think you've had enough adventures for one night.'

She looks troubled. Perhaps her mother had been right; maybe he'd been unwise to talk of the Narclops just before bed.

'There's nothing to worry about, our species advanced. We grew beyond ourselves,' he says, stroking her hair.

'But what if the Narclops are still there, inside all of us, just... waiting?'

'The Narclops won't come back. We won't make those mistakes again, not here. Remember: *There Is No Self.*'

He kisses her furrowed brow and wishes her a good night, closing the door quietly behind him.

She sits up, restless, and presses her face to the window beside her bed. Out there, somewhere, is that strange planet Earth, playground of the primates, necropolis of the Narclops. She tries not to think about them, tries to concentrate on the two moons that shine like beacons outside the window, her breath catching in her chest as she whispers, *There Is No Self, There Is No Self* over and over again. But all she can see is the face in the glass staring back at her.

# The Lost Children of Lorenwald

by

Elizabeth Hopkinson

# The Lost Children of Lorenwald

Every forest tells a story.

Broadleaf or pine. Sunny or tangled. Autumn or spring. Each forest has its own unique song to sing, its own tale to tell. And it is the craft of the Storysinger to gather those tales and sing them to whoever will listen.

It was neither autumn nor spring when I came to Lorenwald, but the lazy end of summer, when fruits hang heavy on the raspberry canes and the sunset sky is abuzz with tiny wings. I was too early for the cider harvest, but I drank my small beer in the common room of the tumbledown inn, and nodded my thanks for the plate of cheese and black bread.

'What brings you to these parts, aunty?'

The hostess wiped her hands on her apron and watched me eat with scrutiny, no doubt waiting for my reaction to her home baking.

I smiled. In this part of the country, every woman of my age was 'aunty'. Once, I had been hailed as 'daughter' but those days were far behind me; a few more years and I would be 'gammer'.

'I go into the forest to collect songs,' I said. 'I'll give you a tale or two from other parts after supper.' I patted the hurdy-gurdy that lay on the bench beside me. 'I expect you don't get news very often in this neighbourhood.'

In most local taverns, this offer was usually met with a roar of approval, along with requests for popular ballads and love songs. Here, the only sound was the thud of a tankard on the table, as every pair of eyes in the room fixed a cold stare in my direction. Even the wasps seemed to stop buzzing.

'No one goes into the Lorenwald,' said the host, his voice like granite. 'By Order of the Village Council. It is a cursed place.'

'Forgive me, I don't mean to cause offence.' I took care to smile as I spoke. 'But I have walked many, many woods in my time. I know their ways as well as you know the art of brewing. Most supposed curses and hauntings are simply a misunderstanding of nature's ways. I have never encountered anything more dangerous than a boar or wolf. And I am well equipped to deal with those.' I showed the horn and knife at my belt.

The host's expression never changed.

'No one goes into the Lorenwald,' he said. 'We lost our children there.'

*

Children get lost in the woods. It happens. In their innocence, they stray from the path, only to fall foul of the elements, wild beasts or – God forbid – unscrupulous humans. When it happens, it is a tragedy that can tear out the heart of a community. I knew that well enough not to press the host and hostess any further that night.

But to avoid the forest because of that tragedy is to seal off part of the heart and to refuse to let it grow again. I could not leave the village without at least trying to set it on the road to healing. So I told the hostess I would stay a few nights and I offered simple songs for my keep: harvest carols that fitted with the season, full of fruitfulness and plenty. Tales of sorrow would keep for now.

In the morning, I went to the churchyard. I wandered among the graves in the golden glow of dawn. There were child graves, as there always are. Such is the way of life. But there was nothing that spoke of unquiet rest or the kind of communal trauma I had sensed in the common room.

When the sun became hot, I retreated to the cool and

shade of the church. In most ways, it was like other country churches in these parts: whitewashed walls, a covered pulpit, simple pews. But between two of the windows was a memorial plaque in bas-relief, the like of which I had never seen in any church. It depicted youths and maidens dancing as they might do on a May morning, their heads crowned with flowers. On one side they were smiling, showing coy pleasure in each other's charms. But on the other side, their expressions became glassy. Trees plucked at their clothes and overshadowed their heads with branches. At the extreme edge of the picture, the young people could no longer be seen. A tangle of trees hid them from sight.

Beneath the image was a simple inscription:

*To the children of Lorbeerwald, now called Lorenwald.*
*The forest took them.*

*

Over the next few days, I questioned people as subtly as I could. A chat with old wives as we washed our clothes together at the village well. A tale of old times with the blacksmith's aged father, in exchange for news of distant lands. Some were as stony as the tavern host, refusing to speak if I so much as mentioned the forest. With others, a torrent of words gushed forth, as if their mouths had been dammed for years. A beloved daughter. A treasured son. When the young people had taken to the woods on May Day, as young folk did, their child had left the group alone, never to return. It was thirty years ago. Six-and-thirty. Twenty-five. One woman whispered in my ear that her daughter had been the last, nineteen summers ago. That was the year the Village Council had declared the forest a forbidden place. A man not yet thirty showed me the brand on his left hand that he had received for snaring rabbits. He had only been trying to feed his family, he told me. His daughter could be out picking berries in the Lorenwald now, were it not for the Council's ban.

That evening at dusk, I crept as close to the eaves of the Lorenwald as I could without being seen. Unlike the depiction on the church plaque, the trees were smooth-barked and graceful, with wide clearings in-between. The last of the day's sunshine cast golden pools of light on the forest floor. The perfect spot for dancing – and for other pleasures that might follow. I smiled; my own youth seemed very distant now, but I had not forgotten.

Perhaps the young people had simply run away together? A secret tryst in the woods, perhaps with youngsters from a neighbouring village, and then away to a new life? This did not seem the kind of forest where a youngster could lose their way, especially a local lass or lad familiar with its paths.

I crept closer. Already, I could sense the edges of a song, reaching out towards me. There was peace in its voice, stillness, serenity. I frowned, struggling to catch it. Another level was hidden behind the first, older, deeper. A struggle? Fear? Flight? If only I knew more!

A twig cracked behind me.

'Curfew has already tolled, aunty.'

The host's face was a stony mask. I nodded my head and followed him back to the inn.

\*

I had to get into the wood.

A forest's song can only be heard when you stand under its canopy, its earth under your feet, its scent in your nostrils. I waited until the sky had turned to the mauves and sapphires of a summer's night, and the villagers were all abed. They were country folk, working hard and rising early, hoping to make the most of the morning's light. They would sleep soundly.

I took a dark-lantern, checked the knife and horn at my belt, and made my way along the overgrown path to the Lorenwald. A few milky stars showed in the deep blue overhead. It was an enchanted night, a night made for young lovers.

The song I had heard on the eaves of the wood grew stronger as I walked beneath its shade. Peace. Fulfilment. Freedom. This was not a story that had ended in tragedy, whatever the church plaque said. But there was something else that had come before. Something the youngsters had come to the wood to escape. They had begged the trees to take them in. Had I heard that aright? Gently, I put my hand on the green-grey trunk of an ash tree. The energy beneath my palm was palpable.

*Tell them.* Was I imagining these words? *Make them understand. Our choice. Our lives.* I had never felt energy so powerful. Was the spirit of the lost children somehow within these trees? I moved my hand to a neighbouring trunk. The song was the same.

*Tell them we miss them. Make them understand, Storysinger.* The cry was becoming more urgent. Make them understand what? That the children of the Lorenwald had gone... where? *Tell them, this is who we are.* There was a vibration in the ground, a rustle of foliage in the distance. Someone was coming. *Tell them, Storysinger.* I had minutes left. I took out my knife and cut a dry branch from the base of the trunk.

Not a moment too soon. Lights were bobbing through the forest. A few breaths later, and I could see the faces of the host and several greybeards, stern-faced beneath their hoods.

'You will come with us, Storysinger,' the host said. 'You will pay the price for breaking our law.'

The branch in my hand wailed.

*

A court had been set up in the inn-yard. The host and six others – the Village Council, I presumed – sat at a long bench at one end. The other villagers sat at tables with ale mugs or watched from the stables. Playing children were shushed and scolded. This was a serious matter, and most of the faces showed it.

I could hear my own heartbeat as I rose to give my defence. The penalty for entering the wood was branding. Not only would I be unable to play an instrument for months, but the brand on my palm would mark me out as a criminal wherever I went. I would lose the only livelihood I had.

I toyed with the dry branch in my hand. All night, I had been whittling away at it, as much to keep away fears as for any notion of how I might use it. It now had the form of a rustic flute, hollow inside with holes for mouth and fingers. A speaking flute. I had heard of such things in tales. But could a makeshift flute speak in such a way that any but a Storysinger could hear it?

I licked my dry lips.

'My good host, members of the Council, good people of Lorenwald.' As a Storysinger, I had been trained to make my voice carry, and now every head lifted. 'I will not make excuses for myself. I know I broke your rules. I simply ask that you pay attention to the voices of your own children, who left this village for the sanctuary of the Lorenwald. They were not stolen from you, as you suppose. Neither are they far from you now. Hear their song.'

I put the flute to my lips and breathed life into the dry wood. I barely knew what I expected to hear, but the voice that came forth was one I will never forget. Sorrowful and serene, gentle and pure, it was the voice of the forest itself.

*Forgive us, dear parents, if you cannot understand. We grew up among you, but you never truly saw us. While our companions longed to unite with each other as one flesh, we wished only to preserve the intactness of our own bodies. When you spoke of your hopes and plans for our marriages, we feared the bridal chamber. When the Rites of May drew others to take our hands, to speak to us with words of desire, we were afraid. We begged the sheltering forest to let us in. Our prayers were answered. Before our pursuers could catch us, our bodies were ringed with bark, our fingers turned to foliage. We became free to live our lives intact, graceful and growing.*

*Do not reject us, dear parents. Do not forsake us, although we are changed. Walk among us once more. We will shelter you. In life and death, we will watch over you. We are your sons and daughters: Haldis, Gyda, Armand, Nordika, Elrod...*

As the litany of names sang out, one after another of the villagers crossed themselves, fell to their knees, wept on each other's shoulders. When the song ended, I lowered my flute and was silent. I looked at the host. He sat with his head in his hands, sobbing like a baby.

\*

I left Lorenwald a few days later. My pack on my back and my knife at my belt, I took the road down the valley, headed for the next village eager to welcome a Storysinger.

But not before I had witnessed a sight I will treasure all my days. Men and women, their hair grey with age, walking under the eaves of the Lorenwald. Some walked hand-in-hand as couples; others walked singly and alone. Most had tears in their eyes. I saw a light of recognition in their faces as each approached a particular tree. I saw them embrace the grey-green trunks, kiss their lost children, sit beneath their shady boughs. Before I left, many an aged parent had taken up the strains of an old lullaby or well-loved tale.

It will be many years before I visit Lorenwald again. When I do, the villagers will no doubt call me 'gammer'. The old folks I left beneath the trees may well lie buried under them. But I will not forget what happened here, when the lost children were found once more.

# Iron Man

by

Claire Stephenson

# Iron Man

The first time she sees him he is little more than a stick figure doing jumping jacks in the distance. Line, cross, line, cross, a signal blipping on the horizon path across the top of the park. She watches him as she crumbles bread for the pigeons. Beaks pecking onto her fur-lined boots. He is too far away to notice her wrapped snug inside thick brown layers on a wooden bench cast in shadow. Pigeon throats flash purple and green as they scuttle and thrust. She does it on purpose, draws them this close. She likes an audience for her tales.

The man is running now, bright orange shorts and vest can be made out above thighs as big as the trunks rooted around the circle where the old woman sits. Soon she can hear his grunting. She eyes him up as he drops nearby into press-ups of impressive variety and duration, winks at her as he gets up and begins stretching. He is amicable enough. Chatty and limber, thinks she might be lonely. This interaction with him might make her day, her week, her year. She is nothing more than a little old granny and he is the big bad wolf still feeling the rush of adrenaline.

He pretends to flirt with her, tells her about his next iron man competition at the weekend. She can sense the triple potency of the triathlete. Watching him she feels like moving again, a sudden impulse to skip.

She flatters him back, 'Ooh! If I were a girl again I'd chase you for a lap or two.'

She sees him struggle to imagine her sacklike shape as an upright hourglass with flowing locks and a face smoothed into the reflective surface of the young. Her face now is terrain, not something to show him back to himself but something that demands attention, vista, solidity. Landscape formed over millennia containing more stories than she can hold.

'Iron man,' she mutters, rubbing her hands together with glee and releasing them with a flourish of fingers surprisingly long and agile.

He doesn't hear her, distracted by a sudden cramping in his calf. He moves to stretch but finds his limbs heavy, his tissues congesting. He is thirsty. He wonders how he can be so dehydrated after his second isotonic energy drink. She watches his pose twist into something quite magnificent. A look of total concentration on his face, the detail of vein bulging on neck and forearm.

*

The next day a young woman is sitting on that same bench he'd put his feet on while he dipped and clapped in between executing strong movements controlled as much by pride as muscle. She is tossing chunks of bread into the air. The gulls dive and swoop it away before the pigeon cloud mobilizes. Their empty beaks desperately tapping out Morse, dot dot dot, dash dash dash, dot dot dot. The woman is talking to herself. There's no one around, just a circle of trees, some birds and an iron sculpture of a man. Orange rust nicely contrasting with summer's still green end, it hints at autumns coming. She looks forward to brisk walks, seeing her breath in the cold air and being warm enough to enjoy it. She trails her fingers over the statue, stops to look it straight in the eyes. She inserts a pink flushed nail under a flake of rust on his cheek, places it on her tongue, savours the metallic taste of blood. She pats his bicep. 'Iron man indeed!' she whispers, standing intimately close. She sniffs his oxidised surface, inhales him. She winks, turns and walks away. Gives a skip, allows a giggle to rise out of a throat long used to cackling. She doesn't look back.

# Airless

by

NJ Ramsden

# Airless

I used to love watching the sky machines when I was a child. We'd walk across the plains, my parents and I, my hands raised up into theirs, my steps unfirm, distracted by the shadows. The paths were good then, the ways clear of the debris that conflict would eventually bring. I'd stare out at the horizon, watching the clouds grow slowly upwards, dark, solid-seeming, like slowly rolling smoke. It was not smoke, of course, it was breathable air. My childish mind did not understand it then, and there is much I do not understand now; I may grasp the mechanics of it, the processes by which a technically hospitable atmosphere can be generated given the right base materials, the right environment, the right human population, the right planet. I suppose the problem was never going to be the technology. The technology is often the easiest part to understand.

My earliest memory is of my mother bathing my younger sister. I was three years old, my sister was a newborn, and we lived in a small and simple house in the Second District. Back then, most homes still had small plots of land and some sense of privacy. Back then, we could still afford to play in the yard, making spaceships from boxes, using our childish handsets for sending breakable codes to each other; as we grew, all that was stifled, and with hindsight, it was being stifled as my sister splashed incoherently in the lukewarm water my mother had drawn into a plastic tub and was gently sluicing over my sister's awkward, thinly haired head.

'Isn't she beautiful?' my mother asked as I watched.

I didn't know what to say. I had never considered beauty. I was three years old, and the subtleties of abstract concepts were only just forming in my young mind – and yet, a nascent sense of propriety had already taken root, the sign of a good upbringing I suppose some might say – so quite blankly, and with no sense of conviction, I said 'yes', and my mother smiled whimsically down at her new fat pink daughter, and my sister plashed and chuckled, and I stood by, passive and watching, with only a vague understanding in my heart that somehow, in the end, all this would pass away and be forgotten. And yet, it is that first moment, and others like it in my young life, that I return to now, when all seems lost, when all truly seems to be at an end, when the hope I once had that something of that vanished life could be retained, and nurtured, and grown again – it is those intangible moments that I reach out for, grabbing what I can and setting it down, as though the recording of information still matters. The sky machines are failing, and a vicious uprising has battered any dreams of a stable future on this rock; the Anti-Reformation League, dead set on undermining utopia, have seen to that. We are dying, slowly, as the air we had made runs out; and I am dying, rather more quickly, as my body leaks its struggling blood into the red soil.

My mother always read us stories. My father had done so, once upon a time, but had been called away on duty, and never returned. My mother spoke of it only once, on the morning he left: 'Your father is leaving,' she said, and that was an end of it, at least in conversation. I wept, and have wept a great deal for it since. Once I thought I heard his voice over the network, but it might have been static. The atmosphere out here is thin, even after years of terraforming, and the mixture of gases does peculiar things to one's senses.

We'd inherited books – actual books, physical slabs of inked-upon paper, crumbly and dry as they were, the boards curled, the edges scuffed, the pages sometimes barely hanging on. I have no idea where they came from, some long-dead relative perhaps; certainly they weren't something my parents would have bought, not on our credit. Some were technical volumes, wonderfully obsolete and therefore fascinating. We would laugh at the specifications of old-time computers, feign shock at the waste of georesources, nod sagely as the eternal wheel of politics turned a familiar face once more; and we would smile at the predictions they made of a future that could not come soon enough, and in some ways came too soon. Other books were story books, and those my mother would read to us, as day gave way to blackout. Most of the names are lost to me now, and the stories have drifted into fragments that, like the shadows of clouds, are indistinct yet palpable; they are felt, rather than remembered. One particular book, however, does remain clear: a book of fables and myths, a book bursting with febrile and haunting images, their tangibility no less for their flatness. There were drawings of strange creatures, and tales of their exploits; of ghosts, of great black beasts, of tiny mischievous humanoids that would roam the byways of the ancient wooded world. I still feel vividly the hairs on my neck rise as I recreate these stories for myself; they help the lonely sleep.

My sister and I were separated: first from my mother, in the standard colony procedure, once we had both attained our merit certificates; and then from each other, as we reached Independence. I had expected more ceremony, but I quickly learned how little interest there is in abstract performance out here on these distant settlements. Independence was just another marker in our lives, along with birth, merit, breeding, and death. The training we had for manning these atmospheric gas converters – the sky machines, everyone calls them, with a wry nod to romanticism – was focussed, intense, and punishing. Earthers often dismiss the colonists as untamed but the opposite is true – we are highly regulated, dedicated to the technicalities, and tolerate conditions even Earth cannot claim in its faded state. I was assigned to comms control, and in weather like this – in what passes for weather, as fierce and monolithic as it is – comms control is no desk job. You might expect the tech at these outposts to be cutting edge, testing the limits of what is possible – but really, the limits are still painfully human, and the tech is obsolete, and hard to source, and tough to fix. Lika, my sister, was assigned to compositional analytics, so the only training we had together was the generic colonists' survival routine, infrastructure maintenance, all the basic emergency procedures. Our mother was downgraded from service early owing to a degenerative illness not uncommon amongst colonists; her muscles atrophied, her mind slid away into darkness and solipsism; eventually, in the face of medical indifference, she died. Usual practice is to compost those who die 'healthy' – old age, accidents, suicide – but illness is a taint our biosustainability targets do not need, so the bodies of the sick dead are compressed into blocks, sealed, and ejected across the compound's perimeter into the wilderness. It seems a disrespectful end, even in this desperate place.

Life inside the station is hard enough, as viable land grows more slowly than the population it must support – as those modest, dreamlike homes of my youth, with their windows and small yards, become windowless slabs – as the traversable open spaces between buildings are filled with ad hoc structures to house more people, broken machinery, the goods necessary to keep these systems alive. Our domes have been at capacity for too long, and the strain has brewed dissent, fuelled on both sides as each accuses the other of stealing from the plant. But nothing is that simple. We suffer constant storm damage, dust erosion, acidic fallout as the atmosphere shifts unwillingly from one state to another; and we wake to holes ripped in the storage basins, punctures in the outer rim, shattered panels in the sheer domes where no colonist would dream of climbing. Some blame the weather, others each other; and some of us think silently of the darker, stranger world in which we are mere intruders.

Those assigned to extraboundary duties have long brought back tales of unidentifiable marks upon rock, of things half-glimpsed as wayward light moves over rough surfaces; they talk mutedly of strange sounds that echo across the dunes, of the hairs upon their naked skin bristling to a sense too primitive for cognition. They speak mostly to a kind of uncomfortable derision, to a dismissiveness born of fear – and I listen, as those who have been out there alone listen to each other, and tell them the stories I remember from my childhood books, of fairies who would steal travellers away, of will-o'-the-wisps who would lure them to their doom. We laugh about it, then, as though these stories, so often meant for children, are childish. 'These things are too big for fairies,' they say, smiling weakly as they consider the length of a human stride. A chuckle will ripple briefly around the room, and decay into silence. We all know someone who has vanished beyond the relative safety of the compound. Secure zones are marked on everybody's maps; surrounding them, swathes of blankness peppered with obstacles. The surveys are ongoing. The drones do not always return, data loss is frequent. Lika, drafted into a drone recovery team beyond her remit, was separated from her group in grim weather. It was said that interference had jammed her comms, and she simply walked the wrong way. She never came home.

I checked the logs surreptitiously at a quiet terminal, and read that her final calls for help had been fragmented and senseless. They said the prolonged exposure to our undeveloped atmosphere had reduced her brain function and she had effectively suffocated, helmetless, her small backup breather – pragmatic for short expeditions, lacking the capacity for long hauls – having expired. I downloaded her last transmission, and played it so many times I barely need to hear it now to experience it.

[LOG START]

L: I... I'm not seeing you, Recon. Confirm location, over.

[noise]

L: Recon, confirm location. Over.

[noise]

R: ...ka, we're hea... base, the sto... vy, maintai... n, crew on w... over.

L: Recon, I... wait, I...

R: ...ing for you, L... ver.

L: Recon?

[noise]

[noise]

T+30

L: Recon, I can't... air... airless out here. Preserving. Out.

[noise]

T+57

[noise]

[background interference; unidentified atmospheric disturbance]

L: ...con. I see you. So beautiful. This shadow. Reminds me of... I once dreamed about sunlight. They say it played on rivers of clean water, back on Earth. I saw pictures... those stories, you know, Mika... oh! So light! It's... no, wait... no! NO−

[LOG END]

We do the best we can in the face of continual hardship. I was assigned to a problematic sky machine out in the desert. It would have been half an hour by skimmer, but their engines kept failing out here; so I took a buggy, which took half a day to tumble its way awkwardly over the boulder-strewn sands. The skies out there are immense – great stormy oil-dark clouds barrelling across the firmament, flumes of green spiralling upwards from their depths as unnatural pockets of gas combust in lightning. The storms wander but never stop; on clearer days, it is possible to see the mountains rising up in the far distance, the walls of our valley rising to a vast plateau before them. This is where our sky machines are sited, but even in the calm and clear, they are difficult to spot, dwarfed by the geology. On darker days, when the clouds are in, when stepping outside means bearing the oppression of the very stuff we were aiming to breathe – on these frequent, long, dark days, everything is invisible. On these days, we rely on our navigation tech, on our memories of small reliable features – a rock here, a fissure there – and on hope.

I remember rolling across the plains in my battered, ageing vehicle, suspended in its cockpit amid balloon-like wheels. I had read in those old books of sailors, people who would throw themselves at the mercy of Earth's oceans in vessels made of trees; I had read their stories of sirens that lured them onto rocks, of mermaids that swept them down to their doom; and I felt, on my solitary journey, much as I imagined those long-dead, buffeted by the elements, sick from the ceaseless turbulence.

Time passes oddly out beyond the perimeter. It ceases to be a constant, measurable by the mundanity of the countless minor operations enacted by others, and becomes a variable, flexing like a band one way and the other as the isolated mind finds ways to distract itself, or not. The vehicles that pilot themselves are notable offenders in tripping the trap of introspection; always better to steer the thing yourself, and have something to focus on for fear of driving into a crevasse. The hours went by, I cannot say how; and then, in the dimness of the hanging skies, I saw my machine.

It leered out of the rolling clouds like a black wish emerging from hatred. The machines of that iteration are vast pyramids of some obsidian alloy that would suck the gleam from a diamond; they are like holes, spaces in which the material of the universe has simply disappeared; and they are eerily silent, operating on principles beyond my ability to explain. They work on the air around them, sucking it in at the base and pouring it out at the peak like a volcano.

My job was to repair an intermittent communications link that fed data back to base; it was the weak link in the chain, something about the process caused local disruptions to the electromagnetic field and surges would rip through the delicate old circuits and fry them just enough to be trouble. The data link, needing clearance, had been placed as high as possible; I would need to climb the machine to gain access. As I trundled towards the pyramid along the gently rising valley floor, it grew ever larger through the glass, and my view became ever dimmer.

I drove for a long time between first making visual contact with the machine, and reaching the plateau upon which it sat. I parked the buggy nearby, disembarked, and with my breather firmly in place and my tool bag shouldered, walked the short distance to the towering black façade. The air at the base of these machines is cold, and moves quickly. There is no danger of being sucked into the ports, but the movement generates moisture on surfaces, making them slippery and damp, and sometimes a thin mist will form across a moderate radius, which the pyramid gradually ingests, pulling more mist from the air around it. In other circumstances, I would risk the opinion that to watch this happen is beautiful; pragmatism paints it a nuisance. My legs were chilled right through as I stepped onto the rungs of the ladder that ascended the machine's sheer slope.

The best way to scale a tall ladder is to clear it from your mind. Do not think an angled climb is easier than a vertical one; tools and breathers become encumbrances, dangling awkwardly, colliding with knees and elbows. The rungs are always too narrow for comfort, spaced a little too closely to use every step, a little too far apart to take two at a time. The panels on either side are smooth, glassy, featureless. I have never managed to count the number of rungs on one of these ladders; there was a joke that became a rumour that became colony folklore, that there was never the same number of rungs twice; that the object itself shifted to defy prediction, to unsettle certainties. If anything was certain in the vicinity of the pyramids, it was that very sense that nothing was quite how it should be.

It is impossible to tell, on a dark day, exactly how far up the pyramid one might be; when the storms move on, leaving a pocket of relative tranquility, the distance is all too obvious. No one starts a climb like this in bad weather, but it can worsen quickly, and at those times the best move is to clamp yourself to the ladder and wait. The storms are perpetual, but they move on. That day was clear enough to start with, but the clouds were low and shifting. As I mechanically cycled my limbs, grabbing, releasing, breathing, and trying not to count, the world around me melted into haze – then, gradually, imperceptibly except with hindsight, shrank into nothing. It was just me, and the ladder, and a metre or two of black pyramid in any direction. Gravity here is not quite Earth gravity, but near enough that things don't sail away when you throw them; enough that climbing a long way is hard work in thin and slightly unstable air. Enough for accidents to hurt.

Eventually, the red glow of the pyramid's vent burned through the fog up ahead. The data link access panel lies within spitting distance of the upper rim, where the silence of distant observation becomes a seething, sibilant exhalation. The density of the gases here is such that concentration becomes an effort after a short time, and breathers are advisable for long procedures; I took mine off, preferring to acclimatise while I assessed the damage. The hatch was easy to open, and the modules inside were in good visual condition. I took some probes from my pack, loaded up the schematic, and started the usual tests.

At first, everything went well – it looked like a simple new-for-old swap would be the simplest way to deal with things – but when I searched my pack, I cursed my stupidity as I realised I had left the parts in the buggy. I would have to go all the way back down, and up, and down, again.

The descent was tedious, tiring, and frustrating in equal measure. When I got back to the buggy, I could not immediately find the parts, and had to root around amongst bric-a-brac and kludges to find a good module. It was my own fault. I should have prepared adequately. It would have been easy to blame the scarcity of good parts, easy to blame the dissenters for looting, easy to point at the damage to the compound and say, 'this is why I am failing, this is why I am not a better man', but I knew better; so I gathered the things I needed, and took deep breaths, and went my way back up the interminable ladder.

Perhaps I took to those rungs too quickly, too ardent with misdirected anger. Certainly I wanted this job done, as already I had spent long enough out here alone, and the weather was closing in tighter, the clouds descending to the plateau and thickening as I scaled the machine, muddying my perception further. Changing out the data module was tougher than it should have been; I was becoming exhausted, my breathing laboured, my limbs aching. As the storm winds crept up, I carried on heedless. Why I did not clamp on the ladder, I do not know. The job was nearly complete, I only had to reconnect the jumper leads; I must have done so clumsily, as a great spark leapt up and blinded me, searing my hands. It threw me from the ladder, and I fell.

I remember little. I fell, tumbling down the pyramid with no sense of direction; only the relentless wheeling of my body as I hit the rungs and spun off, bouncing down, and round, and down. My tools, my probes, my screen, my pack, no longer things of utility but of danger, as they swung around and collided with my knees, my chest, my face. I spun, and I reeled, and I tasted blood, and that was all I knew.

And then it stopped.

Even now, I cannot say clearly what happened; after all that has passed since, after all the violence and recrimination, after all the pain we have caused each other, after all the time I have spent with this in my mind, I cannot say how I survived. My eyes were stabbed with pain from the blowout, I was concussed – and somewhere on the face of that black metal mountain, amid the fog and the fumes and the collision of altered molecules that filled my weakened lungs, I felt a hand.

Something stopped me from rolling to a broken doom on the rocks beneath the machine; something slowed me, and carried me down, and I remember trying to open my aching eyes, but I could not see; only a piercing light in the rolling grey haze. I was laid on the ground – I felt that much, felt the pinch of uneven rubble against my back, felt the slow run of thick blood into the back of my throat – and I must have lost consciousness then.

I remember waking. I remember sounds like ripples in

water, like the giggle of a small child as it plays. I remember turning my head on the bloodied dirt, and opening my eyes at last.

There was light. Two shapes, neither human nor entirely inhuman, long limbs, small bodies, large heads, protuberances upon their shoulders like wings, but not wings; they glowed in the buggy's headlights, which I had not remembered switching on. One was rifling through a sack of things, taken I suppose from the cockpit. The other stood away, by boulders, and against the light I saw with this creature another, darker being, a shadow only; and that shadow saw me, and stopped in its gesticulation; and it came towards me, step by measured step. I closed my eyes from the pain.

I heard the shuffling of boots on dirt. In a moment, my head was lifted slightly, and cushioned on something soft and warm; a hand smoothed my hair; a soft and human voice spoke my name.

*Mika.*

I opened my eyes, against the agony of seeing.

'Lika... Lika...'

My sister sat over me, her long hair spilling out from around her like a halo of warmth; but she looked thin, and pale, and white, her skin almost translucent. Her voice was as beautiful to me as ever.

*Mika, you're badly hurt. You may die. We need to get you home. Come with us.*

'No... Lika, no, I just... they need me... the base...'

*Shush, Mika. I understand. Don't worry.*

Lika wiped my face with her warm hand and I felt the mask of a breather descend upon my mouth, trapping weak words within it. My eyes closed. Everything was agony. I heard voices again, Lika's voice, and that lapping, liquid sound. Then silence.

I woke on a trolley in a medical suite, the grey walls and dented old equipment a familiar sight. My eyes felt better, my head was sore but not terrible, my hands were swollen but flexed with little enough pain. A tube led from a small pump of some kind into my left arm. After a while someone came in.

'Good to see you awake, Mika. How do you feel?'

'Not so bad,' I said, unexpectedly hoarsely. My throat was rough, breathing slightly awkward. My chest began to throb.

'You broke a couple of bits and pieces,' said the medic, 'but you'll be fine. We put your things in a box on the side there.' She nodded to my right, where a small white tub sat next to a bottle of fresh water. 'Take a look through, if you can move your arm okay. I'm going to fetch someone you'll want to see.'

Lika, I thought. But no. That's ridiculous. She disappeared a long time ago. I reached across to the tub, but was clumsy and knocked it to the floor. I swore.

There were footsteps in the corridor. The medic appeared again, briefly. 'Someone for you,' she said, and went away.

A moment passed. A tall, thin man stepped into the doorway. Not Lika. My father.

He looked tired. He looked old. For so many years I had seen only pictures of him, pixellated footage of vanished days. Neither of us spoke. He came up to the bed, bent, and picked up the heap of things I had sent down. He placed the tub back on the stand, and passed the rest from hand to hand.

The medic came back in. I was glad of the interruption to our awkwardness. She adjusted some settings on the pump and raised the bed slightly at the head. 'That's what we found you with,' she said. 'You were lucky. When you didn't come back, we thought you were gone like the rest, but then we got your distress call. You left it quite late. Better care next time, eh?' She winked, smiled, and left me with my father. We looked each other in the eye for the first time in over two decades.

'I didn't make a distress call,' I said. 'What have you got there?'

My father handed me the contents of the tub: an ID card, some half-eaten and rather unhappy-looking rations, and a small square of metal on a rough cord. I didn't recognize it.

And then I did. *Åse 1273*, it read: my mother's ID. I looked at it for a long time. 'It can't be true,' I said at last, and handed it to my father. 'It's her plaque. From when she died. It was out in the desert,' I said, looking to my father for credulity, waiting for truth, and sense, and meaning.

'I didn't know,' he said. 'I was a long way out.'

He sat on the edge of the bed, and we held hands, and I wept like I had not wept in long, dry years.


I still don't know what really happened. I do not know if Lika is out there still, or at all, and whether I had not dreamed all these things in some madness; but the plaque speaks for something. I suppose she found it, one day, and was able to live amongst those creatures, whatever they were. We have no name for them. When I was well again, I told my comrades what happened. They teased me, and laughed, and said with some sorrow and not a little humility that Lika had gone to live with my fairies. It began as a joke, became a rumour, and settled into colony folklore; now everyone knows the story of Mika and the mountain, of Lika and the fairies, of how they rescued him; now everyone leaves trinkets out on the plains when they are called on expeditions. I am something of a local hero for my stories. The children love to hear them.

Sadly, I must go now. The fighting is too near, my injury too great, and my console access is about to come to an abrupt end. I only hope these Earther insurgents, when they find me in this wreck of a shelter, realise what they have destroyed. I hope they realise, some day if not now, that the hope of

something better is what carries us through, not the fear of it –
and that hope, amongst other things, is to be found within, and
nurtured and grown from the stories people leave behind
them. When all else is gone, when all that is left of a life is a
tale or two, what better than to dream them back again?

Meanwhile, the Earth is dying, and now too this small
colony; when the sky machines sigh their last sighs, I hope only
that Lika lives on, as perfect as always and as best she can, in
this hard, airless world.

[LOG END]

# The Daughter with Indigo Eyes

by

Moira Garland

## The Daughter with Indigo Eyes

I am not looking for another baby.

In the early twilight, from within the ruins of the house comes a cry, so small I might have missed it. Few are left who know me, yet this tiny voice speaks my name, *Annie*. Close by, the *carrkh* of a loitering raven quarrels against a curdling autumn sky.

Daily I make my brick-fields pilgrimage – jagged houses blinded by the bombing, empty gaps where windows, doors or even walls once stood. They console me, reminders that others have suffered too, I am not alone.

Clambering over the threshold in my old court shoes, I pick my way over the dusty floor, avoiding the ghostly litter beneath the ruptured roof, towards the corner shadows where a heap – darker, cleaner, paler – emits a damp forest decay.

A nest of sticks, lumps of grass and moss, a soft lining of sheep's wool, cradles a naked infant, a girl-child who first smiles then squawks. A flap-flapping almost knocks me backwards – two ravens fly away to a perch atop the house walls. I peer at a fine-looking baby: curly hair as dark as a winter midnight, golden skin, deep blue eyes which follow the flight of the birds, before settling on my face.

While I am not looking for another child, how could I leave this one all alone, unloved, deserted?

I gather her up, hold her close to my own warm body, inside my threadbare grey coat, a match with the surrounding rubble. I must keep this infant safe. Hurrying away from the rough nest I reach my own house, the fire banked up in welcome.

I name her Cora.

What better life could Cora have? In these rationing days I stitch together her dresses, cut from discarded adult clothes.

My frozen fingers tug off the kale leaves, turn over the sweet-smelling straw piles to pull out carrots and swedes for our little family to enjoy home-cooked Irish stew.

On the swing built from old pieces of wood, free bomb site booty, Cora reaches heights that terrify other children.

Passing the brick field acres on the way to Cora's school, I relate her foundling story; she listens, looks wise, asks questions. I am pleased that her voice has now softened, is the voice of a girl, no longer the knife-sharp baby cry. Cora is my own daughter, a daughter whose skin glows lustrous against her black hair. In the way that mothers do I often gaze into the depths of my daughter's eyes looking for love or some such sentiment. Time and time again I see only a flinty glaze.

My dearest wish is that she should be happy.

*

On a balmy spring afternoon I unfold the deck chair, then settle down to a novel. A single *carrkh* from overhead disturbs me, evoking the day I discovered Cora. I have not told her what drove me to the brick fields that day and so many other days: images of Arthur dead and buried in the desert sand. That was to be the worst of my woes, I thought then. In the expanse of half-obliterated houses I relish the serenity, away from the bustle of the shops, the ordnance factory, the din of children in the school playground.

'Was the film good?' I welcome Cora home from *One Hundred and One Dalmatians*, her thirteenth birthday treat with her best friend Jeannette.

'Not really.'

Perhaps she is old enough to see *A Taste of Honey*, perhaps I should have given way, perhaps she is dreaming of a wilder life, perhaps she is a Jo. I still peek into her bedroom when I know she is asleep, her arms outspread, in her pink baby-doll pyjamas. Perhaps she dreams of flying off...

Cora has indeed grown to be a dazzling young woman but one of turbulent spirit.

'Fetch some more coal for the fire, love.' I resort to eggshell tones.

'Why is it always me?' Cora stomps out, swinging the empty coal scuttle.

Banging the door shut on her way in, she clanks the metal scuttle on the hearth, defies me, glowering.

I try soothing her. 'You've got coal dust on your lovely new red skirt.'

Her hands sweep over her miniskirt, but the marks remain. She dashes upstairs. In double-quick time she has slipped on a black crew-neck jumper and matching black skirt. I know better than to say *Not black again, you should be wearing crimsons, bright blues, canary yellows, at your age!*

\*

Many an evening I ask, 'Where are you going now?'

'Out.' The door slams.

In the insomniac hours I wait for the click-click of the front door key. Unwanted images waylay me: *Jeannette distracts the corner shop owner while Cora snatches cigarettes; Cora boards a bus into the hills above the town, her cigarette smoke disappearing in the wind, while she fingers her jet-black hair falling below her shoulders (even in the coldest frost, or snow, when others wrap up in warm coats, long woollen scarves, cosy gloves and the latest knitted hats she keeps her hair uncovered, smoothing it to a gloss); Cora swoops down the hills into town, hair fanning into wings ready for flight; a young man sweet-talks Cora at the Creation Club, 'You're a gorgeous bird. Do you know your hair turns red and green under the lights?' Cora upright, proud, 'Yes, I am, and I do.'; Cora stares from behind an iron-barred window... while a solitary violin scrapes out a soundtrack in a minor key.*

\*

Saturday mornings are generally a quiet time. Cora is upstairs sleeping off whatever has passed the night before. A February sun frets outside. *What Do You Know?* drones on the Light Programme. I am cooking the midday dinner, listening, trying to answer at least some of the questions when I catch the tap of footsteps down the stairs, so I stop my carrot-chopping, lean through the hall doorway. Cora, in her protective black ankle-length coat, holding a bulging leather suitcase, has reached the bottom step.

'Where are you going?' I trail her to the front door.

'I don't belong here!' She tears off, through the gate, swinging the case, round the corner into the next street, too fast for me to catch. She is gone.

I wipe away tears, the other hand grasping the gate. Of course the ravens, unkind, have gathered above me.

'What do you want with her? You gave her to me!'

They hang in the damp air, then vanish, bequeathing the rumble of a car and the yapping of a dog further up the street.

\*

The police do not find Cora. I do not change her bedroom. Fears surface in the night of never again seeing my daughter, of never setting eyes on her shimmering skin and hair as dark as my despair. Despite attempts to corral my fears I take again to wandering the brick fields, haunted by Cora. Grief and death are longstanding friends whom I cannot forsake as I recall the cold satiny skin of our first little daughter, crushed before I could reach her bed in the bombing that rained down on our city night after night.

So as each of Cora's birthdays passed I had conjured up a happy-ever-after, fairy-tale ending.

*

One baking hot afternoon, my roaming done, my legs aching, I find the front door unlocked.

'Who's there?'

'It's me.' A distinct voice from the front room.

Cora, a grown woman, strangely smaller in height, stick legs planted firm on splayed feet. Her hair is as straight as my vegetable rows, layered, shinier, reaching right down her back. I am shocked to see her skirt, jumper, tights, shoes all faded to a beggarly grey, and giving off a low elemental whiff. Yet the air pressure shifts upwards. She looks happier than ever, unaware of her appearance.

'Mum, I've been away so long.'

'My Cora.'

She takes my hand. 'Let's have a cup of tea. Get the deck chairs out, we can sit in the garden.'

So Cora tells me a tale of drugs, a gun, hospital, prison and friends who turned out not to be friends. Then a kind woman who took pity on her at a railway station on a night when even the birds froze, who took her home, fed her, gave her faith back in people, hope in what she might be.

'So have you found what you want to be, Cora?'

'You always wanted me to be happy, Mum.' She shifts over towards me. Her indigo eyes glitter. 'If I'm happy will you be too?'

I will always remember these words for at that instant I hear again the *carrkh, carrkh, carrkh* of a sleek, ebony-black bird gliding overhead, its bluish-green head radiant in the sunlight. I turn back to Cora. In her stead stands another magnificent raven. All at once, croaking over and again, the two birds take flight, soar into a high blue sky. Sinking back into the deck chair I track their heavenward path, their illuminated feathers transmuting to silver.

\*

When summer comes round again I pick off caterpillars from the cabbages, offering sacrificial bounty for the bird table. Obedient, famished children, heeding their mother's bidding – *Come in now, tea's ready* – the returning raven pair feed on the mini-banquet. One dips her head – a nod to me. Then, counting on a mother's constancy, they take wing.

# Flower-Face

by

Ness Owen

# Flower-Face

After his mother's three curses, Lleu could have no earthly wife. She denied him a name, weapons to defend himself and the chance of human love that she so desperately craved for herself. His uncles, who raised him as their own, were able to break the first two curses through trickery and their powerful sorcery but the last curse, being driven by an absence of love, had defeated them. So with no other hope, Lleu's uncles set to create a wife for him. She would be crafted from flowers: noble oak catkins, delicate meadowsweet and gracious broom. And their creation would be named Blodeuedd – woman of flowers. Yet in their marvellous crafting, Lleu's uncles had overlooked nature's order: no one is born a grown woman.

This is where I began. Who remembers their own birth? I was unable to forget the terror of being thrown into a world of rules that I didn't understand. Born into bewilderment with no mother's milk to soothe me. An infant girl lost in a woman's body.

As all infants do, I watched and learned from the uncle sorcerers as they did as they pleased, and took what they wanted; they quite forgot that I was watching. I married him I was given to just as I was told. The uncles proclaimed that such a striking couple required a great kingdom and we were given the kingdom of Ardudwy. Castle fortress, fields and forests, sheltered by mountains and shouldered by the relentless sea. Lleu was as kind as he was handsome. I had no reason to complain. He treated me graciously and it was easy to fall into the role of a dutiful wife. The court was content, the land prospered and the harvests were plentiful. I was surrounded by the joy of others.

Yet Lleu grew homesick for his uncles who had treasured him as every child should be, and he longed to see them again.

He kissed me goodbye and promised he would return as soon as he could.

Our room was colder after he left although I grew to enjoy the silence. Left to fill my own days, I wandered around the court until no corner was unfamiliar. I sapped answers from my maids and guards until they could no longer respond to my relentless questions, but my thirst for knowledge was still untouched. As the days grew shorter, I grew braver. Leaving the castle walls, I explored further into the kingdom.

Outside, the flowers whispered to me. *Come with us. Come with us if you want to live.* At first I skirted around the forest, being careful to keep the castle walls within my sight. But the whispers became louder and their scents filled my nostrils, waking me from my dreams at night. I could ignore them no longer and followed the pathway to a flourish of broom and meadowsweet. Sweet and heavy scented, they brought me to a place before memory: to warmth and contentment and home.

All at once, a lifetime's sadness fell at my feet and my mind raced with questions. Unspent anger burst through my skin and softened my bones and I lay down amongst the flowers and listened. They spoke of their gifts of serenity, light, honour and showed me how to bend with the forest-winds and to learn to love the rain. They told me I must walk further but the path had ended.

'How will I know which way to go?' I questioned. The answer rang in my ears. *Let your feet find a new way.*

Steadily one step followed another. My eyes opened to greenness and my ears opened to each fresh birdsong. I walked until I reached a magnificent oak whose branches reached out to welcome me. I bowed before her. She told me that one day I would understand the secret of her strength and find the power of choice. When the time was right I left her and made my way back to where I was before.

I felt the thunder of hoofbeats before I heard the hunting horns. Louder and louder they came from all directions and my steps turned to strides. The faster I ran the further away the castle seemed but I knew I had to reach the grounds. Gasping for breath, my legs weakened as I shouted to the guards, 'Someone is coming. Pull down the gates!' They ran to greet me, telling me it was only a neighbouring lord.

Crouching near a window, I watched the passing group. It was at that moment, in one held breath, that I saw him and my heart fell open. There wasn't a part of me that didn't long for him and I asked the guards to call him in.

His name was Gronw. Sun-weathered and strong, he was a worthy hunter. Later, we greeted each other in the gardens. I offered him my hand. My skin tingled at his touch and his breath quickened at mine. Unable to hide our thoughts, we talked through three nights about the impossibility of our love.

'One thing is certain,' he said, cutting a lock from his hair and placing it in my hand. 'We'll have no peace while Lleu still lives.' He left with the promise that he'd return if I could find a way to free myself of Lleu.

I awoke alone to the news that Lleu was coming home. They dressed me to meet him at the gates. He was pleased to see his wife and I wondered if my eyes would betray me but he saw nothing but a reflection of himself. The journey and the separation from his uncles had exhausted him and in no time he was asleep on my lap. I waited till his breathing was deep and slow and then softly placed his head on a pillow. Brushing my hand through his hair, I caught a few strands with my marriage ring. Light and golden, I placed them on my palm, along with Gronw's dark lock. Putting them in a handkerchief, I slipped away into the forest.

The path was easily found and I picked blossoms of broom and meadowsweet along the way. Returning to the oak, I placed the flowers and the strands of hair at the trunk and pleaded, 'What should I do?'

I listened but no words came. Disappointed, I begged again. 'Please, I need to know.'

A forest wind whirled around me, sweeping up the flowers and locks of hair. Circling the trunk faster and faster they merged into one, pulling me towards them. The oak's branches creaked above me. Flower pollen fell like a rain mist. Unable to see, I reached forward for the oak to steady me. The ground shook and rumbled beneath me but I held on to the oak. When at last the ground settled, I opened my eyes to see what was before me: earth, light and water – all that I needed. My kingdom was here.

I understood that I, the flower woman, finally had a choice. I turned my face away from the castle and let my roots sink back into the earth. Each day my skin darkened and I grew taller, stretching higher towards the light. Look and you will find me, the tallest oak in the forest still growing; gracious broom and delicate meadowsweet at my feet.

# Spawned

by

Clair Wright

# Spawned

Just last week in a hospital not far from here, Ruby gave birth to her first child.

Ruby lay on her pillow in an exhausted fog, her red hair stuck to her forehead in sweaty straggles. She watched the midwife as she bustled about, clearing away the bloody aftermath. In her stained apron she looked like a butcher. This was not how Ruby had imagined it. Not at all.

Her husband Ricky wept with pride, great tears spilling from his eyes and drenching his shirt. He gazed at Ruby, seemingly unaware of the carnage around him. He wore a wide grin.

The midwife handed the baby to Ruby, efficiently wrapped in a bundle of blankets. Ruby pulled back the edge to look into her baby's face for the first time. It was crumpled, angry, and green.

'A healthy baby boy!' declared the midwife.

'He's beautiful,' murmured Ricky.

'He's green,' said Ruby, and began to cry.

'He'll grow out of it,' said the midwife.

'He's beautiful,' whispered Ricky.

'He's green,' said Ruby, and sobbed into the blanket.

'Six pounds three ounces,' said the midwife, as she wrote on her clipboard.

'He's beautiful,' said Ricky, stroking the baby's green cheek.

Ruby pulled off the blankets, and the baby rolled naked onto the bed. His eyes sprang open, large, bulbous and yellow.

'He's got webbed feet, and webbed fingers, and he's green,' said Ruby.

The midwife continued to write. 'Webbed feet,' she intoned. 'Webbed fingers.' She licked the point of her pencil.

Ricky stroked the baby's palm and the long green fingers wrapped around his like weeds.

'He's a frog,' said Ruby. 'Our baby is a frog.' She covered her face with her hands.

The baby opened his wide mouth and began a throaty yowling. Ruby gave a wail.

The midwife sighed. She pursed her lips. 'You are a mother now. You have a job to do. He is a healthy baby boy, and I expect he's hungry.' She pushed the squirming green baby onto Ruby's breast and held him there till he began to suckle.

'I told you – perfectly healthy.' The midwife pulled the door shut firmly behind her. She marched on to the next delivery.

Ruby looked down at the baby as he fed. She felt her skin shrink from his green strangeness.

Ricky tucked a spare pillow under the baby. He wrapped the blanket back over his naked body. 'We don't want him to get cold, do we?' he murmured. 'Why don't you hold him tighter, to keep him warm?' He coaxed Ruby's arm to cradle the child.

Ruby pulled her arm away and turned on Ricky. 'Why didn't you tell me? Why didn't you warn me this could happen?'

'I didn't know,' he said. 'Look at his feet! He'll be an amazing swimmer!'

Ruby screamed and hurled her pillow at him.

'You told me you had changed! You told me the curse was broken! Changed by love, you said! You lied to me!' Her pale cheeks flushed red and her blue eyes flashed with anger.

'I did change,' he said. 'Your kiss broke the spell. You know it did.'

'My mother warned me,' Ruby sobbed. 'She told me people don't change, not really. I should have listened to her!'

'But I did change,' said Ricky. 'Look where I'd be without you! Still swimming around in the dark, in the bottom of a well! You rescued me.'

'I thought it would be happy ever after,' she said. 'I thought you were my handsome prince. I tried not to notice when you licked dead flies from the windowsill. I never complain that your touch is so cold, and our bed smells of pond weed. I washed and washed the sheets, but it hangs round them like fog,' she said with a sob.

Ricky winced.

'I should have left you in that well,' Ruby said. 'You and that stupid ball. I should never have kissed you. I should never have married you!'

'You don't mean that,' said Ricky.

'Nine months!' she went on. 'Nine months of sickness, and tiredness, wallowing around like a great whale! No wonder I craved seaweed, and samphire, and oysters. I was carrying a frog!'

The baby stirred, and Ricky stroked his cheek and murmured soothing little sounds.

'Didn't I love you enough? Is that why? Is it my fault?' Ruby sobbed again, and tears streamed down her cheeks.

'Of course you did, of course you loved me enough,' Ricky said. He laid his hand on Ruby's arm. 'You made me who I am. But deep down, there are some things that stay the same, I suppose.' He stroked a long finger against the baby's green head.

Ruby looked down at Ricky's head bent over the baby. His hair was an uncertain colour, not brown, not blond. The colour of ditch water, Ruby thought. I should have known.

Ruby wiped her eyes on her sheets. 'I dreamed our baby would have auburn hair like me, and blue eyes, and rosy cheeks,' she said. 'I dreamed he would be a perfect baby and I would be a perfect mother. I never thought it would be like this.' Ricky handed her a tissue and she blew her nose noisily.

'He's our baby,' said Ricky. 'He's ours to love. I know you can love him, like you loved me.'

'But what if I can't love him enough?' Ruby said.

'It will be enough,' said Ricky. 'Here, hold him.' He unfolded the blankets and tucked the baby against Ruby's bare skin. He nestled against her warmth, and opened his eyes.

Ruby shrank from his wide yellow gaze, but she held him still. In the pools of his eyes she saw reflected her own blue ones, and her auburn hair.

'Hello baby,' she murmured. She bent and kissed him gently on his damp, smooth head. And as she looked at him, he seemed a little less green, already.

# Bearskin and Bare-skin

by

Carys Crossen

# Bearskin and Bare-skin

My foster-sister is a brown bear, and I was named after her. My name is Ursula, which means *bear*, and my ursine sister was christened Bernarda. According to our mother I outdid my sister in grumpiness, sleepiness and appetite until our third year.

Our father, poor man, was an unsuccessful hunter. He knew the woods and the valleys, none better, but he lacked the ruthless edge needed to profit from death. Besides, he was never a good shot. But his gentle grey eyes and ready smile won our mother's heart completely, capricious soul that she was. My mother was a henwife, a wise woman, one of the cunning folk, and they lived together not unhappily in a little thatched hut at the edge of their beloved woods.

I was born along with the springtime. A mere three or four days after my birth, our father came across a dying bear. She was lying beneath a willow, every futile breath an agony. Our father put her out of her misery, and then to his consternation found my sister huddled under the bear's great forepaw. She had fur, and her eyes had prised themselves open, though she was toothless, biteless, helpless.

Our father took the cub back to our mother. She nursed me, still nameless, and the cub at her breasts, and from then on we were sisters, Bernarda and I. She gave me my name, and was my earliest friend. We slept in the same crib, played on the same hearth, suckled at our mother's breast together and were closer than any human girls could ever have been. Our understanding and love for one another existed before words and was beyond words.

The first blight on our happiness came when we were five. Our father took ill, lingered for several pain-racked weeks and then died as he had lived, quietly and without attracting undue attention. Some men from the village dug him a grave and dug it deep, which was lucky, as more than once Bernarda tried to dig him back up.

Our mother wept without ceasing for a week, while Bernarda and I huddled together for comfort, not quite understanding what had transpired. When hunger sank its teeth into our bellies, we wandered into the woods, seeking out nuts, berries, and honey that Bernarda scooped out from a beehive for us, while the bees buzzed round in annoyance. I scuttled up trees like a squirrel for apples and pears, and for a time we lived as wild creatures in the woodland. We were not lonely, for we had each other.

Eventually, our mother had no more tears to shed, and we went back to live in our hut at her behest. She made a decent living working as an herbalist and healer, but her broken heart never fully healed. She was forgetful, subject to strange whims and fancies and uncertain of temper. She began to frequent the local tavern, seeking oblivion in strong drink and the arms of a man. None of her lovers lasted long, however, and the grief she displayed at their inevitable abandonment seemed out of all proportion, for though some were decent enough more often they were rough, greedy and hard.

Bernarda and I were now the daughters of a whore as well as a witch, according to the local gossips and the prim, self-righteous village folk. I was a wild thing, a simpleton, a whore-in-the-making also, they would say whenever I ventured into the market for food or leather or soap, voices pitched loud enough so I could hear distinctly. They grew angry when their words had no effect on my composure, but truly, their bitter words meant nothing to me. The buzzing of the bees had warning in it, but their mutterings were like the clucking of puffed-up little hens, all voice and feathers.

And no one ever worked up enough nerve to lay a hand on

me. Oh, a couple of the local bullies tried once or twice, but they always came off worst. Bernarda taught me how to bite, and scratch, and snarl without compunction. If that failed I soon learned where was best to slash at with our father's old hunting knife, which I used as Nature had failed to equip me with claws. After I almost gelded three of the village boys I was left alone and was quite content to be so. For I had Bernarda, always had Bernarda, and she had me.

And then the villagers turned on my sister.

*

We were ten by the time the villagers became truly dangerous. Not that Bernarda ever harmed them, or their stupid fat pigs and goats, or even dug up their gardens for roots. She had too much sense for that. I had taught her that humans were troublemakers. Of course, by that time I did not consider myself human, nor did Bernarda. We both thought of me as a strange hairless bear. Bernarda never made me feel my inadequacy, but inwardly there burnt an ember of shame at my weakness and uselessness compared to her.

For by our tenth year, Bernarda was a beautiful big brown she-bear, with claws like steel knives and jaws that could snap a man's thigh-bone like a twig. The villagers worked themselves up into hysterics about what she *could*, what she *might* do to them and one blustery night came to our hut, with fire and knives and shotguns.

Bernarda and I heard them coming. We roared our defiance, but there were simply too many of them. They set fire to the thatch, screaming for Bernarda's blood.

We ran to the back door. It bordered the wood, and a quick glance outside confirmed the villagers had left it unguarded. I told Bernarda to run, run fast and run far. I would have gone with her, but our mother lay insensible on her bed. Neglectful drunkard that she was, I could not leave her.

'Run, Bernarda! I will find you.'

I went back for our mother. It was as bright as hell in our home, the heat like a living thing that wrapped itself around you and tried to suffocate you. I dragged my mother free of the flames, out through what was left of our front door. The villagers, only minutes before screaming, livid, bloodthirsty, went silent. A dead bear was one thing, but a dead woman would bring questions, lawgivers, magistrates, their landlord, the hangman.

They left. Our hut burned to cinders. Our mother died, just after dawn.

And Bernarda was gone.

*

I combed the woods for days, searching for her, but my sister had vanished. I would have searched forever, but one day in a fit of remembrance I ventured back to the ruins of our home to bury our mother. I found her already buried, next to our father in an act of thoughtfulness that shocked me. I also found the local lord, on whose land the villagers dwelt. He hauled me onto his horse, took me to a convent, tossed the nuns some gold for my dowry, and, his duty towards me done, rode back to his great house to hang a few sundry villagers for their misdeed.

While it would be gratifying to tell that I immediately ran away to find Bernarda, or that I burned the village down in an act of vengeance, it would also be untrue. I was still a child, heartbroken, weary and confused, and I acquiesced to whatever the nuns wanted of me. I was fortunate in that the sisters were a true religious community, and treated me with patience and kindness.

The endless religious services were a bore, as was prayer, and they soon gave up trying to make me look demure. My hair defied even the starchiest wimple, and the smocks they put on me never stayed clean. As for habits, the only one I developed was stripping naked and sunbathing in the herb garden, which nearly gave a visiting bishop a conniption on one unfortunate occasion.

But there were compensations. The nuns were scholarly women, ardent followers of Theresa of Avila and Catherine of Siena. I learned to read, and to write, and to speak French and Latin, and the principles of mathematics and rhetoric, and even a little music.

Whenever I had a spare moment, I could be found in the convent's library. I read about the saints in times past, most particularly about Francis of Assisi, and St. Corbinian and St. Romedius and their saddled bears, about St. Gall receiving firewood from a bear, and every day I thought of Bernarda. I read the works of the great Augustine, and his musings on transmogrification and its impossibility, and wondered if he had it right. I read stories about demons, witches, wolves, and wolf-men and men-wolves, and wondered if a human could be turned into a wolf, then why not into a bear?

*

When I was fifteen it was miserably apparent to everyone that I had no vocation for the spiritual life. The sisters lamented my loss, but made no attempt to force me into an existence I was so patently unsuited to and I loved them for it. They gave me some food, a little money and a copy of Hildegard of Bingen's *Physica* and turned me loose. I left the sisters, and went to find *my* sister.

I returned to the woods. I was resolved never to leave them again. I lived as the saints did, amongst nature, except I wasted no time on prayer and meditation. Every day I sought my sister, but not only her. For in teaching me to read, the nuns had given me knowledge, and more importantly, had taught me how to find knowledge.

The knowledge I sought was how to change my shape. Humanity held no attractions for me, except for their books and I could live without those if I had to. My heart was with Bernarda, with the woods and the wild, and always would be. I wanted to be a bear, a true bear, not a hairless mimic. With that in mind, I sought out those who might be able to help me. I sought out fools, tricksters, wise men and women, witches both false and true. I ventured to wherever books could be found, and scrolls, and writings, and scriptures. But the knowledge eluded me.

As did Bernarda.

One night I dragged myself back to my shelter, heartsick and footsore, weary beyond all reckoning and half-starved. I fell on my bed of leaves and moss and promptly had a vision.

The beautiful woman at my bedside smiled down on me tenderly.

'I am here to help you,' she told me. 'Now –'

'Are you the Virgin Mary?' I asked her.

'If you like,' she answered impatiently.

'What if I don't like?' I queried, puzzled by the answer. The beautiful lady rolled her eyes in exasperation.

'Then call me Hecate, Titania, Brigid, Gaia, Hera, Morrigan, Cerridwen –'

'I like that one,' I interrupted.

'Very well,' answered the beautiful lady, heaving a sigh of premature relief. 'You may call me Cerridwen.'

'Are you real or have I gone mad?' I enquired interestedly.

She actually stamped her foot in irritation.

'Does it matter? I'm here to help, you contrary thing!' she shouted.

I decided to remain silent.

'To business, then,' the lady pronounced imperiously. 'You wish to turn into a bear, and I am here to tell you how.'

'Go on then,' I prompted when she paused impressively. She shot me a glare that could have etched glass and continued.

'Bernarda is not far from here; she lives in a cave next to a waterfall,' the woman continued shortly. 'She is the one who must help you. You look human, but you know you are not. Bernarda is the one who will turn you into what you truly are. Find her.'

'And then?' I whispered. The lady eyed me critically.

'She's skinned tougher quarry than you,' she said dryly. 'A few good rips should do the trick.'

'Or I'll die in agony,' I muttered.

The lady shrugged.

'I didn't say it would be easy – or safe,' she said with a sigh. 'It's up to you. But from what I've seen of you, Ursula, I think you'll take the risk. Good luck, Bare-skin.'

Without the least transition I was lying on my bed of moss, utterly alone. I might have dismissed it as a bout of hallucinatory madness, had it not been for the footprint stomped into the earth next to me.

*

I found Bernarda.

She was right where Cerridwen told me she would be. For a moment I stood frozen, as I watched her dip her muzzle in the pool at the waterfall's base so that she could drink. She was larger and more beautiful than ever, and I was terrified she would not recognise me, would have forgotten me, would resent me for leaving her for so long.

Then I gathered my courage and called to her, and it was as if we had never been apart. Bernarda came racing to me, scooped me up in a bear hug, and we rolled across the ground. We embraced, we cried, we explained and traded tales and caresses. She had run for miles in her unthinking terror, and had lost herself. She had searched for months to find familiar woods and valleys, but until today had never seen any trace of me.

Strange to say, but it had never previously occurred to me that my being able to talk to Bernarda or she being able to talk to me was anything out of the ordinary.

Once we had exhausted ourselves with talk and emotions we slept for a little while, and then I woke Bernarda and explained what Cerridwen had told me.

It took me a long time to explain things (Bernarda had no truck with visions or hallucinations and other such nonsense) and even longer to persuade her to take the risk. Bernarda, like all true bears, was of an immensely practical turn of mind and skinning was something done only when prey was dead. Skinning a living creature was not something she had ever considered, and the mere suggestion of doing it to her sister, her long-lost sister, was a travesty of the highest order.

I persuaded her. It took a long time. The leaves on the trees had changed colour, fallen and regrown before she gave in. (Bernarda, unlike other bears, had never picked up the habit of hibernating.) Then one day she heaved one of her great sighs, and gave in.

I hugged her one last time, and then she raised her great paw and tore my skin from me with one horrifying blow.

My skin sloughed off as a snake's would. Skin, hair, teeth, nails. I was excoriated, peeled, pared. I was flayed alive and it was bliss.

I did not bleed and it was over in an instant. I roared in agony and ecstasy commingled as I stretched my spine to its full length, reared on my hind legs and then embraced Bernarda in a clumsy bear hug.

A real bear hug.

*

We live in the woods, Bernarda and I. You couldn't tell us apart, save that my fur is a shade lighter than hers. We are not the truest of bears. A little of our old human selves and lives bleeds over into our present existences. We do not hibernate. We outwit even the canniest hunters, and the convent where the nuns sheltered me has a pair of ursine protectors that deliver the nuns safely through the woodlands and valleys even in the harshest winters or when the highwaymen are abroad.

I never saw Cerridwen again. Why should I? Her work was done. I wonder sometimes who she was, why she helped me, but Bernarda tells me not to bother my head with mysteries when there are roots that need digging up. Always practical, Bernarda.

But above all else, we are happy.

# Crossing the Victoria Line

by

Marie Gethins

# Crossing the Victoria Line

On good days, the stationmaster let her sing near the platform, winked when she crawled under the turnstile. She'd told him about her mum, dad and those social workers who didn't understand. Voice gone, she'd try to travel today, sleep in the heated carriages that went up and down the Victoria Line. Brixton to Seven Sisters and back. Bright blue on the Tube map, almost the colour of her mother's eyes.

No one called the girl by her name. Not since her mum died. But the girl remembered her mother's name, Victoria. She heard it in the clicking of the tracks, the rumble as the train went through tunnels. She wondered if her mum could see her shivering.

The girl waited in the station doorway. Still too early for normal people, the streets remained empty, cars still. Grey clouds pressed rooftops while snow flurries swirled through orange streetlight skirts. She watched the glowing dance line of poles until they began to flex and sway. The girl closed her eyes. Sweat froze on her forehead and a cough rattled her chest.

Canvas trainers, wet since the beginning of November, squelched as she shifted from one foot to the other. Hours earlier her dad had given her head a smack, pelting her out of the high-rise flat with blackened spoons and a crushed paper cup. He had the agonies coming down after a bad bundle. The dole money spent. 'Get out. Earn some buff, Girl. Sing and fill up that cup.' Her lungs ached. When she swallowed, her throat burned.

Wandering the streets during the night she saw her mother. The girl peered through bay windows and watched her nurse babies, play with toddlers, hug dads that popped off billboard ads. Christmas trees still lit. Paper streamers hanging from ceilings.

The girl slid down the wall, leaned against the metal station gate, and curled into a corner. Her foot struck something. It skidded a few inches across the concrete. She leaned forward and picked it up. A pink lighter. The girl held it towards a streetlight beam, shook it. The clear fluid almost reached the top. Her dad always wanted lighters for his rig, told her to nick them from the corner shop. Instead she picked up what she found around bins and doorways. A full one – a surprise for her dad. She wondered if he might leave off about the empty cup.

The girl coughed and blew on her stiff hands, cupped the lighter between her palms. She ran a finger along the wheel indents. 'Just once,' she said aloud. The girl pressed her thumb against the black lever. A click, a hiss and a small flame quivered. She stared at the soft white light rising from a blue core. The girl saw an open fire inside the lighter flame: a fierce blaze dancing around a pile of logs. Heat spread across her shoulders, face and scalp. She stretched out her feet and steam rose from her trainers. A gust blew into the doorway, snow engulfing the flame. The lighter slipped out of her hands. It landed with a clatter.

She scrambled onto her knees and searched the rough ground. The girl grabbed the lighter and rolled back into a corner, knees to chest. She pushed the black lever again. The metal wheel rasped – once, twice and then a flame flared. She spun the adjustment ring, it grew higher, wider. A large dining table appeared lit by candles. Roast turkey lay in the centre, surrounded by bowls of potatoes, Brussels sprouts and stuffing. A crystal dish held cranberry sauce, the red berries glinting like rubies. The girl's mouth watered. She could smell roast meat. Her fingers became hot and she let go of the lever. Sucking her fingers, she thought of turkey but only tasted salt.

Snow continued to fall, but the sky lightened. Orange

streetlights snapped off in timed order. She heard the hum and bottle chime of a milk float far away. London rising from its slumber. Soon shopkeepers would tell her to move along. She clicked the lighter again, increasing the flame height to maximum. The yellow-white flame became hair, the dark blue centre eyes. 'Mummy?' The blonde hair looked thick and glossy, not the thin strands the girl remembered. Eyes bright, whites clear without red veins. The image smiled – her teeth lustrous and even – not grey and pitted. 'Mummy?'

The lighter spluttered. 'Please take me with you. Don't leave me here.' A ball of warmth crept from the girl's stomach, through her limbs. With one hand, she pulled off her shoes and unzipped her hoodie. The world slowed. Staring into the flame, the girl felt arms embrace her, lift and carry her into a clear light.

*

The Brixton stationmaster found the girl as he opened the gate. 'No, God, no.' He checked for a pulse, then tucked a strand of hair behind her ear. He thought of the many times he had watched her sing for commuter coins tossed into a paper cup. Now she looked peaceful, and for the first time, he saw a smile – frozen on her face.

# The Salt Child

by

Rachel Rivett

# The Salt Child

Once there was a child made completely of salt. Her skin was smooth and cool as crystal and her hair sparkled white in the moonlight. But the Salt Child wasn't happy for she had no friends in the big busy City. The people there had soft squishy hands and their streets and their shops and even their clothes were a chaos of crashing colours. 'No,' she sighed. 'This is not where I belong. But if not here, then where?'

So she set out to look for a place that would look and feel and smell and sound like home. She walked in the cool moonlight until she came to a forest. The trees bent to greet her and the rush of the wind through their leaves whirled a wild song of freedom around her. Her heart raced.

'It sounds right...' she murmured. Looking down she wriggled her white toes in the dark crumbly mud. It smelt of damp earth; of dying things and growing things; of death and life and... a cycle she didn't quite feel part of. Reaching out she grazed her salt fingers against the bark of the trees. How hard it was! How solid! How rough! An ant scuttled onto her hand, turned a dizzy frightened circle, and skittered off as fast as its many legs would run.

'No,' she sighed. 'This is not where I belong. But if not here, then where?'

So, she walked and walked until there were no more trees; she walked on as the days grew hotter and hotter and the air burned so her salt arms grew sticky. She had reached the desert. Gazing over the sweep of sand that stretched in every direction all the way to the sky, she felt as if she stood at the centre of a great circle. So much movement! Waves of sand shifting, the air shimmering.

'It looks right...' she murmured.

But then a sharp gust of wind struck her with a stinging

spray of sand. She cried out! The sand stuck to the hot sticky saltiness of her, coating every inch of her arms, her face, her legs. Even her mouth was gritty! She spat the sand from her tongue.

'No,' she sighed. 'This is not where I belong. But if not here, then where?'

She was so tired now, but again she set off. She walked on and on until the air cooled and began to tingle with a scent that seemed sweet and familiar: the salt child could smell wet weed and wild water. She had reached the sea.

'It smells right,' she murmured.

A beat of sound beckoned her like the pulse of a great heart. She closed her eyes and listened to the quick rush of foam and the slow drag of pebbles. A never-ending song of praise.

'It sounds right,' she murmured.

Opening her eyes, the salt child gazed at the sea. It glittered and glimmered, a thousand shades of blue and green and aquamarine, luminous and alive. 'It looks right,' she said softly.

'Ah,' she said, smiling, as she stepped into gentle waves that tickled, licking and lapping her toes.

'Ah,' she sighed, as she stepped in deeper and the cool clear water hugged and held her like a friend. Slowly, the salt child began to dissolve, each particle mingling with the shining salty sea. Oh, the lift and shift of waves! The shimmer and shiver of it! Bliss!

'Yes,' she murmured, raising her arms and twirling and twirling until her dance and the sea's dance became one. 'This is where I belong!'

# The Truth About Tea

by

Sarah Armstrong

# The Truth About Tea

We finally came out of the dark tunnel that ran under London Bridge station. My shoulders relaxed a little, and then I saw the name of the street.

'Crucifix Lane?'

Diane looked at me. 'What about it?'

'Just gives me the shivers,' I said.

Diane half smiled and turned left. I followed her, watching the silk scarf curl behind her. The scarlet matched her lipstick and her shoes. She always coordinated too much.

I couldn't read her well, but I knew she wasn't keen that Alec and I got engaged without consulting her. Summoned to this special bonding night, I was confident I could win her over. Then again, I had also been certain I'd get a good meal out of it, somewhere that Alec would take me. But, instead of driving to the West End, Diane dismissed her driver near Waterloo.

We arrived in front of a tall, soot-blackened building and she stopped. The Truth About Tea, the sign read.

'A tea shop?' My stomach grumbled. I'd turned down a night with Cara for this. We could have planned the hen party and had a chicken kebab on the way home.

'After you, Sophie,' Diane said. I nodded my head, almost a bow, and went first. A bow? She had that effect on me, made me feel so subservient with her steely manner and hidden jewels.

It was poorly lit inside. I could sense someone talking at the desk and I heard Diane give her surname, but my neck felt stiff and I found it hard to look up from the black carpet. The pile was high around the legs of the desk and the toes of my shoes.

We were escorted to the end table in a long room with black and silver wallpaper, lit by red candles. I counted as we passed eleven other tables, each occupied by one younger and one older woman. The paired women stared at each other. They looked deep in conversation, but the room was silent. Our feet didn't even make any sounds on the thick carpet. We sat down and assumed the same position.

A bell tinged, light and deep simultaneously. A silver teapot and two china teacups appeared in front of us. I didn't see who put them there, and I still couldn't turn my head to look. I felt anxious but I couldn't pin it down to anything.

Diane poured tea for us both along with the sound of other teapots. My head was full of questions but I couldn't remember them.

The bell tinged again, and Diane and I lifted our teacups. I normally had milk and it tasted bitter. I shivered, forced myself to swallow and closed my eyes.


I was sitting with Cara. She looked odd, slightly blurry, and I had a strange taste in my mouth.

'I feel weird,' I said. I blinked and she came into focus.

'It's the stress. How are the wedding plans coming along?'

'Well, his bloody mother keeps sticking her nose in. So, as expected.'

I smiled, but her smile took a little longer than usual.

'Are you okay?' I asked.

'I'm just worried about you,' said Cara.

'Why?'

'Oh, you know.'

I wanted to look away but couldn't.

'It's all sorted,' I said. I didn't even convince myself. It hurt and probably always would.

'How is it all sorted?' she asked.

'Dean has gone to Australia, hasn't he? So that sorts it for everyone, I suppose.'

'And Alec? Does he know?'

'No. He doesn't ever need to know. It doesn't involve him. We'll just get married, and Dean will do whatever he does.'

'But you don't love him the way you love Dean?'

'You know I can't love anyone the way I love Dean.' My eyes began to fill and I blinked it away. I forced a wide smile. 'Why are we talking about this? We need to talk maid of honour dress styles. I was thinking something dark, quite rich.'

'Like Alec?'

'What?'

Cara's lips were pulled back. 'Rich like Alec. He's only your second choice, but rich enough to make it worthwhile.'

'Cara, what's got into you tonight?' Was it night? I felt as if I'd been drinking, just slightly off-kilter. I didn't recognise the room behind her, but I'd thought we were at her kitchen table. It was quiet but I had to strain to concentrate on what she was saying.

Cara said, 'You don't love him, do you?'

'No, but when did that ever stop people getting married?'

'Given the choice, would you be with Dean again?'

I hesitated. My head felt strange. I would do anything to be back with Dean again. I would take all of Alec's money and fly to Australia. If Dean would have me, I would sacrifice the world.

'The world. I see.'

'What? I didn't say anything.' But I had the sensation that my mouth had been moving and that the words were still in between us. I heard more words but Cara's mouth didn't move.

'You can't marry him. He deserves better.'

My eyes blurred over and everything was black for a second.

'Cara? Something's wrong. I can't see. Cara?'

Sounds started to build in my ears, the sound of women arguing. Some were screaming in anger or fear.

'I think I need a doctor. Cara!'

A final ting from the bell and I could see around me again. I was in the tea shop and it wasn't Cara smirking at me from across the table, but Diane. Now I could move. Three pairs of women were holding each other's hands and crying with relief or happiness. Most women were glaring at each other, filled with shiny new truths.

I swallowed. 'Diane, I –'

I couldn't think what to say. She was looking around at the older women and nodding to them.

'I was drugged, you forced me to say that,' I said. 'It's illegal.' I picked up the teacup. 'I'm taking this to get it tested.'

She looked at me and frowned. 'You can't steal a teacup, silly girl. Here.' She pulled a test tube from her bag and handed it to me. 'Fill it up if you're sure you want to pursue this.'

'Why would you have a test tube?' I looked at it. 'Have you done this before?'

She laughed. I thought back to Alec telling me about his failed relationships, those engagements that had broken. I'd been glad, and never really asked why they ended. My hand started to shake and I put the test tube down next to the saucer.

I could front this out with Alec, but I knew I'd lose. I would have to move out of his flat, and where could I go? I cut so many ties to get where I was. Dean had gone. I had Cara, but maybe someone had talked to Diane and it could have been her. And then I remembered my credit card with so many deposits on it already. Alec had said he was changing card companies. It was temporary. He'd pay me back. The venue, the flowers, the bloody dress. Maybe I'd be left to pay it all off. I clenched my hands to keep them steady.

'Does Alec know you're doing this?'

She smoothed one eyebrow with a small, manicured finger.

'So many questions, Sophie. I'm sure Alec will answer some of them.' She patted my hand and my ring glittered sadly. 'But the truth about this tea is,' she leaned closer and whispered, 'it's just tea.'

# Girl on a Pied Horse

by

Sarah Hindmarsh

# Girl on a Pied Horse

The darkness roared as the girl on the pied horse fled before it. Hooves thudded into baked earth as tendrils of creeping black curled towards them. The pied horse galloped faster. The girl clung to its mane, her knuckles white. If they could make it to morning they would have time to hide. But morning was a long way off and the horse was growing tired.

The unearthly darkness eclipsed the moon, plunging the girl and the pied horse into blackness. The horse stumbled, the girl almost catapulted from the saddle. She clung on harder as the horse raced blind. A tiny light appeared beside them, flickered for a moment and settled on the girl's knee.

'Where do you run to?'

'We run from the darkness, Wisp, we know not where to.'

'Follow us then.'

A trail of quivering stars appeared on the ground before them. The pied horse sped towards the first, and the darkness howled once more. The girl looked down at her knee, but the wisp was gone.

The wisp lights guided them through the small hours, through the haunts of witches and ghouls, the threat of werewolves and harpies. The girl and her horse knew only the lights, the rhythm of hooves on dirt, and the sound of their own laboured breathing until, at last, a faint yellow glow appeared in the east. The darkness, knowing it had only a few short minutes left, screamed as it flew towards them, reaching recklessly close to the sun. The pied horse swerved, leaving the wisps behind, and headed full-tilt for the dawn.

The girl risked a look over her shoulder. The darkness was falling behind, cowed by the rising sun. The pied horse slowed and then stopped running; sweat dripped from its flanks and shoulders, mixing with the blood from the girl's hands as it stood, trembling, in the light of the new day. The girl climbed down from the saddle and the horse dropped to its knees. Beneath the horse's rib cage its great heart tried, and failed, to steady its rhythm, then something burst. The girl sobbed as the horse struggled to breathe, flecks of blood appearing in its nostrils.

'He gave his life for you.' The voice came from behind the girl. 'Now let us ease him into death.'

The girl stood back as the wood nymphs surrounded the horse. They laid a green cloak over its face to soothe it and hummed a lullaby. The horse ceased trembling. Its ragged breathing slowed, and for a moment became calm and even. Then it stopped.

The wood nymphs stood, joining hands in a circle around the fallen steed. They sang a song that blossomed into the air with an energy that seemed to come from the core of the earth itself. The horse's body sank into the hillside and from the spot on which the noble heart had burst a sapling sprouted. As the chant continued the sapling grew taller, sprouted leaves, then flowers, then berries. It reached towards the sun, growing straight and true until, at last, the wood nymphs stopped their song.

'A rowan,' said the nymphs in chorus. 'The king of trees for the most noble of beasts.'

They turned towards the girl.

'Who are you that this magnificent creature was willing to die for you?'

'I'm nobody,' the girl said, tears pouring down her face. 'I ran from the darkness that was sent after me when I escaped from the dungeon. The horse was my sister's.'

'But it loved you.'

'It saved me. I cannot repay that love in a thousand lifetimes.' The girl glanced at the sky. The sun was climbing overhead. 'I have to go, the darkness will come for me again tonight. I can't let it take me back.'

'Why were you imprisoned?'

'I think it was because I am not fierce or ruthless like my brothers and sisters.'

'Then why are you wanted back?'

'My siblings say I could ruin everything if I am free, although I don't know how.'

The wood nymphs conferred amongst themselves for a minute. The girl watched the clouds changing shape, searching for the spirit of the pied horse in their formations. She found only echoes of the darkness that sought her. One of the wood nymphs held out her hand.

'Come,' she said.

The girl took the hand that was offered, and fell under the protection of the wood nymphs. In a far-off castle the darkness rattled against the windows, filled with rage at the escape of its prey.

'I shall miss Anger,' said the girl as they walked into the forest.

'Anger is not something to miss,' said one of the nymphs.

'Anger is my sister,' said the girl. 'The only one of my siblings to visit me in my prison. The pied horse belonged to her. I didn't want to steal her horse, but the others were all out when I escaped. Only the pied horse was left.'

'And to whom do the other horses belong?'

'My siblings: Greed and Misery, Jealousy and Disease, Poverty and Spite.' She listed more names.

'Hatred and Melancholy returned just as I was leaving. It was they that unleashed the darkness.'

'Who are you?' the nymphs asked.

'Nobody important,' said the girl. 'My name is Hope.'

# Notes on Stories

# About 'Silence Rose from the Water Like Steam'

'Silence Rose from the Water Like Steam' came to me in a feverish rush – starting with an image of washerwomen at a great lake; a silver creature flicking between their ankles. I wrote it longhand, in one go, while the children played nearby. This is often how my stories start their lives.

I wanted to challenge myself to write a group acting as one, rather than a collection of characters. I thought the fairy tale brief particularly lent itself to this approach. I wanted to create the sense of a band of individual women, but with a shared consciousness.

In the story I've explored the collective power of language and how women use it, of ritual and ancient habit. I wanted to write about the preciousness of language, the necessity of giving voice to our thoughts and the effect on a community when communication becomes impossible.

The connection (and disconnection) between words, reality and actions is a subject that is as fascinating to me as it is topical. Perhaps there are no beautiful sea monsters out to steal our words, but there are plenty of reasons silence feels poignant right now.

**POPPY O'NEILL**

# About 'Midnight Riders'

Underground rail networks are often used in films and fiction as locations of interest, but chiefly in crime or spy thrillers, horror, or, in the case of *The Matrix*, to stage a (then-)state-of-the-art sci-fi fight scene. With the sense of all that weight (of earth, of City) overhead, and the crush of crowds, there is often a kind of claustrophobia and tension to be mined from them, especially useful for frantic pursuits. At the other end of the scale, they can be eerie, even terrifying, when empty – who knows what is lurking in that dark tunnel beyond the platform's end? But they can also depersonalise anyone – making them simply a commuter, lost amongst many, just there to journey from point A to point B.

Perhaps it's this last quality that leads to them being taken for granted. I'm not a London local, but whenever I visit, I get the feeling that the Tube has become routine, something to go through, to endure, before work begins, or before you can finally get home and relax. Or before you can go out and (hopefully) have a good time.

The Tube has largely lost its glamour and novelty, is no longer at the cutting edge of inner-city transportation. Its trains are humble beasts of burden now. All it has to do is stay open and try and keep to schedule.

Little thought is spared for the drivers who attempt to do just that. Little positive thought, at least. Nor is much consideration given to what they think of their profession, and what sense of self-worth they can possibly draw from it, when they seem so roundly overlooked – or maligned, in the event of breakdowns or strikes. It struck me that there were echoes of certain peripheral characters in fairy tales (in this case, 'Cinderella'), and the way they simply have a function to complete within the story and are then dispensed with. They are toyed with, changed and then changed back again, used as simple comic foils, and any impact or sense of melancholy or loss that might be associated with these fluctuating circumstances is rarely if ever explored.

I wanted to shine a light on this, in the context of also considering how much our self-respect depends upon the perception of our work – both the ways we view our professional roles ourselves, and the ways they are seen, or not, by others.

**DAN MICKLETHWAITE**

# About 'The Web and the Wildwood'

I love unicorns, but I deplore the pictures that show them as cute horses with horns. It was probably David Attenborough's children's TV series *Fabulous Animals* and the book that accompanied it, a book I've treasured over the years, which first told me the unicorn is strong, fierce and quite untameable. In heraldry it is shown with a goat's beard, cloven hooves and a lion's tail, smaller than a modern horse, delicate and wild. The horn of a unicorn, even the smallest part, can guard you against poison if dipped in water, which is why it was fiercely sought after. The unicorn dips his horn in the water in the forest to purify it for the other animals. Man's hunt for the unicorn violates the balance of nature and puts the other animals in grave danger.

I'm also fascinated by medieval lore, including the gorgeous tapestries that once hung on castle walls, often depicting hunting scenes. There are two sets of medieval tapestries with unicorns in them – 'The Lady and the Unicorn', in Paris, which may be about love, and 'The Hunting of the Unicorn', in America, which probably isn't. The first appealed more as subject matter, but ideas from the second influenced the story I was getting out of the first. Subconsciously I must also have been influenced by Carole King's song 'Tapestry', with its mysterious story of someone being drawn back into imprisonment. The Lady of Shalott, from Tennyson's poem which I loved at school and which inspired several Pre-Raphaelite paintings, became a part of the story when I remembered she was weaving a tapestry too. An internet site suggested the mirror resembled the way we look at the real world through other lenses, not directly. And so my story developed from this fusion of ideas, a story about what it really means to treasure things and people.

**LYNDEN WADE**

# About 'Listening to the Mermaidens'

As a teacher of creative writing I often start sessions with a writing burst, an opportunity to respond to a stimulus without any expectation that the raw material generated will be shared. Sometimes these exercises generate ideas, sometimes only a pleasing phrase or two. But even if the text is never used again, the experience is not wasted. Nothing, I promise my students, nothing we write is ever wasted. And nothing we experience is wasted either. As an undergraduate I wrote a piece for an assignment about a young boy. It was set near the coast, where he inadvertently stumbled across a small boat offloading illegal immigrants. It explored the defencelessness of a young child alone at night and the parallel vulnerability of young men and women exploited by traffickers and abandoned to their fate in a foreign country. When he tries to tell his parents, his story isn't believed. That sort of thing doesn't happen around here.

Years later, in 'Listening to the Mermaidens' I've used a similar idea of a young boy observing a situation he doesn't really understand. In this case what he observes is "fantastical" and his attempts to discuss it are also dismissed as the products of an overactive imagination. But what if he really did see – and hear – a mermaiden? Would he return to the cliff edge and hope to spot her again? Probably. Would he tell anyone else and risk further disbelief and possibly ridicule? Probably not. The image would linger in his mind until he saw her and her like again. He would never forget. He may not speak of them but the mermaidens would linger in his memory until he was an old man. Many of us have experience of elderly friends and family, unable to look after themselves and needing the 24/7 care of residential accommodation. It is often easy, convenient, to dismiss their jumbled memories as symptoms of dementia. The narrator of my story has been ill, after all. He's had a bad fall. He's been delirious. And I never promised you a reliable narrator. But what if the old man really had seen a mermaiden when he was younger? Hush. Listen... here comes the girl with the sippy beaker.

**ANGI HOLDEN**

# About 'Melissa's Bearskin'

The inspiration for 'Melissa's Bearskin' is a ballad from the Orkneys, 'The Great Silkie of Sule Skerrie', which tells the tale of the silkie, a shape-shifting creature who is "a man upon the land and... a silkie [seal] in the sea." I was gripped by the ballad from the first time I heard Joan Baez sing her version of it, back in the early 1960s. I've since listened to and read many other versions, all of them powerful and heartbreaking. Like these ballads, 'Melissa's Bearskin' tells the story of a human woman who conceives a child with someone who looks like a man but is actually another species altogether.

But the ballad of the silkie does not explore emotions – it simply tells the tale. 'Melissa's Bearskin' is my attempt to explore the feelings of the two lovers about each other, and about their child. As well as wanting to explore the idea of "forbidden love" I was interested in the relationship between the human mother and her not fully human child. The idea of a mother who feels there is something alien about her baby is, some have suggested, a powerful metaphor for what many mothers experience when they cannot bond with their newborns, or indeed even before they give birth – it's common for pregnant women to dream of giving birth to a cat or a frog or some other non-human creature. I didn't know when I started writing the story how Melissa would respond to her baby. As the story developed, only one answer was possible for me.

I wanted to look at other themes too – coming of age, and the tensions between mother and daughter; loss and grief. I also wanted to see what happened if I reversed the more common fairy-tale motif of the beast who turns out to be a human prince under a spell.

I'm not sure I would have written this story, though, were

it not for a conversation I had with a very dear friend in New York, Amye Rosenberg. After reading my story 'Lilasette', which was published in *The Forgotten and the Fantastical 2*, she said, 'I want to know what happens to Lilasette's daughter!' I thought about that... and a story began to emerge. So – thank you, Amye. This one's for you.

**RONNE RANDALL**

# About 'The Narclops'

The destructive nature of vanity has been explored in countless fairy tales from the Wicked Queen in Grimm's 'Snow White' to the Lilim in Neil Gaiman's *Stardust*. Narcissism is a vice we are warned against from childhood, yet this seems inconsistent with the world we live in today.

Social media has changed our lives irrevocably. Through our digital profiles, self-interest is positively encouraged and vanity is rewarded with 'likes'. Is uploading a selfie the modern-day equivalent of asking "Mirror, Mirror on the wall, who is the fairest of them all?" If so, then there is a trace of the Wicked Queen in most of us.

I'm curious as to what drives some people to share their experiences with others online in order to gain their approval, their admiration, their envy. And perhaps more importantly, what are we overlooking in doing this? I'm in my thirties, so social media has been around for most of my adult life, but I find it a peculiar thing, and I feel fortunate that I was one of the last generation whose adolescence was not beleaguered by the likes of Facebook.

In my story, I explore what would happen if we allowed our digital lives to overpower us and we neglected to take care of the physical world. What if our virtual narcissism brought humanity to near-extinction? What would future civilisations think of us? A cautionary tale perhaps, but one observed irreverently through the eyes of a child of the future, as she contemplates the bizarre past behaviour of her species.

**SOPHIE SELLARS**

# About 'The Lost Children of Lorenwald'

As with all my short fiction, 'The Lost Children of Lorenwald' was born of several influences. The first was an idea I wrote down several years ago, after watching a TV documentary: "A singer who goes into the forest to gather her songs." This idea stayed in my notebook a long time, unused but available for whenever I needed it. Another important influence was the Singing Bones Podcast on the 'Pied Piper of Hamelin'. (If you haven't discovered this amazing fairy tale resource, check it out at singingbonespodcast.com) The many different historical explanations for the tale of lost children fascinated me. During the creative process, this became fused with two other traditional tales – 'The Singing Bone' itself (I have a thing for magic flutes), and the classical myth of Apollo and Daphne.

Daphne has long been an important figure for me personally. In the myth, she is amorously pursued by the god Apollo, much against her wishes. To escape his advances, she begs her father – a river god – to change her into a laurel tree. This story was one of several that helped me in the process of understanding and embracing my own asexuality. In recent years, I have written a number of asexual stories and fairy tales. I liked the idea of a forest of Daphnes, a silent asexual community in need of understanding. I also like the idea that a storyteller (or Storysinger) is the right person to give a voice to a very real orientation, which remains largely unheard-of or denied in our society.

It was also a deliberate decision to have a middle-aged woman as the protagonist, as they so rarely get to be the hero, especially in fantasy. I like to think the Storysinger will go on to solve other cases in other villages and towns. Perhaps she will.

**ELIZABETH HOPKINSON**

# About 'Iron Man'

I suffer from a chronic pain condition called fibromyalgia. I was listening to a radio interview with Cassidy Phillips, a former triathlete who has the same problem. He made the comparison between how an Ironman looked after crossing the finishing line and a stooped old lady in a supermarket. This resonated for me as a formerly athletic person who often says they feel a hundred years old. Saying it hurts everywhere, all the time, is too strange and vague to help other people understand. I have always wanted to be able to explain it better.

My first thought when I heard the word Ironman was not triathlete. Having lived in Birmingham I think of Antony Gormley's statue in Victoria Square. Maybe this is why I began thinking about a literal iron man after listening to the interview. When I imagined the Ironman transforming into a rusted sculpture it felt so visceral that I knew I had finally succinctly captured elements of my experience I'd been trying to articulate for a while: feeling trapped and unable to move, being physically recognisable as the person you once were yet being fundamentally different, and the enormity of the loss.

Medicine, as yet, cannot cure fibromyalgia but what if it could be transferred to somebody else? Would I be able to inflict a lifetime of pain onto another person? Probably not. Would I be able to do it if they were really bad? Maybe. What if I gave it to someone who was just slightly annoying but had caught me in an unforgiving mood? I found myself empathising with villainous characters in a way I hadn't before.

This transformation tale is not explicitly about fibromyalgia but the writing process was transformative for me. While I may never get to walk away from the pain, writing a character that did was liberating.

**CLAIRE STEPHENSON**

# About 'Airless'

'Airless' began on the Megabus to Newcastle sometime in 2015. I had a few hours to kill, and late November's darkness had turned me inwards. I forget which book I was reading, but I had given up, and on a whim decided to open up my tablet computer and write. Out popped the opening of this story. The name came first and instantly, and the image of the sky machines belching cloud was, I suspect, a kind of persistence of contextual memory from another coach trip to Hull during which we'd driven near a power station and I'd been struck by the blending of the vapour from the cooling towers and the reaching black edge of a coming storm. Once the image was set, I had to fill it out, and where better to begin than childhood?

Some of the matter in 'Airless' is literary. There are familiar folk tale motifs in here, such as the "fairies", the challenging task, the "magical" otherworld (in this case, a strange planet). Setting these off against sci-fi tropes seemed a good bet. There's a similarity, I think, between the kinds of "otherness" found in the villages and forests of folk tale, and the settlements and deserts of a distant world; I think we recognise both as versions of something plausible, yet removed from our own realities enough to render them fluidly symbolic.

And then, some of the matter in 'Airless' is deeply personal. Abstract stories are all very well, but I wanted to flesh out the interior of this piece, to speak of things we know, not merely to signify something intellectual and/or exterior. The bittersweetness of memory and loss, the love of family and the long ache of its splintering, the acceptance of what needs to be done even when just to carry on is hard enough: we all share these histories. In several languages, 'story' and 'history' are the same word, blurring the division of recordable fact and meaningful insight. It was my hope in writing 'Airless' in the way I did to straddle that boundary, to try to blend modes of telling much as the vapour from those cooling towers blended with the storm clouds; to achieve that mixture of something generative, and something discovered; to have it permeate, and become, the atmosphere.

I hope I have succeeded, and I hope that you enjoy it.

**NJ RAMSDEN**

# About 'The Daughter with Indigo Eyes'

Rooted in historical reality, in Liverpool where I spent most of my formative years, and the 'brick fields' – a curious yet accurate name given to bomb sites in the World War 2 aftermath – 'The Daughter with Indigo Eyes' began as a simple "Once upon a time" tale but grew into something more complex with characters exhibiting both flaws and strengths.

A major constituent of this story is about the strength of a woman in time of war, the losses that haunt her and how, despite herself, she cares for another human being and is bold enough to invest in a future. She commits to a new relationship, when she is guided to a baby, and she cannot help but rescue one who has no other human parent.

As a child I heard fairy tales and legends read to me by my mother; from my father came tales of leprechauns. As an adult I read, amongst others, Angela Carter's rich, fantastical tales, and Kate Mosse's magical novel *Labyrinth*. I suppose these have lodged in my subconscious to be drawn upon when writing a story framed in this way.

Two other experiences fed into TDWIE: the legendary brainpower of corvids seen on a TV programme, and raising my own child. At first, in this tale the birds seem menacing, but they trust Annie to both look after and empower a daughter; they choose a woman who will rise to the ups and downs of Cora becoming a teenager and seeking her own path. I hope the story's ending is not read as unhappy – Annie lets go but the connection between mother and daughter continues.

**MOIRA GARLAND**

# About 'Flower-Face'

I was blessed to be raised by storytellers from family members to villagers and teachers. Immersed in stories of both fiction and real life, I revelled in both local folk tales and world fairy tales, often mixing them together.

I first encountered the Mabinogi (four branches of stories from the earliest examples of Welsh prose) when I was about ten years old although I had been aware of images of the characters that I'd seen in paintings and folk tale maps.

It struck me from this young age that the fate of women in the stories was, more often than not, bleak to say the least. They were blamed, shamed and punished. Although there are many strong women in the tales, even these women are almost all constrained by the will of others, often to marry for the good of their kin. They are duty-bound and choice is a luxury not available to them.

This is particularly true of Blodeuedd (Flower-Face). She is created for the sole purpose of marrying and keeping Lleu happy but when left alone she falls in love with another. Her fate is sealed and she must be punished. She follows the instructions of her new love as blindly as she did her creators. Born as a woman not a child, she isn't allowed any time to grow and learn what it is to be a woman. Also, unlike Lleu, who is "mothered" by his uncles (they even ensure that he has a wet nurse for a year so that he grows to double his age), she has no mother figure or anyone to guide her.

Being a 'what if' person, this raised many questions for me. In particular at what point do we change from children to women and what are the consequences of not having a guiding figure? If she had someone to tell her about her own worth would her fate be changed? What if she had the confidence to make a different choice?

As she was made of flowers, it followed that her mother would be the nature around her and there she could be nurtured. A new story began where I gave her a guide, time to grow into womanhood and I waited to see her bloom.

**NESS OWEN**

# About 'Spawned'

This story had been rattling around in my head for a while before I committed it to paper. I am fascinated by what is just outside the frame of a fairy tale – the minor characters who are left behind early in the story, or the lives that continue after the "happy ever after".

When I read the story of 'The Frog Prince', I wondered what happened to the couple after they were married. The princess in the story despises the frog before he transforms into a prince, so much so that in traditional versions it is when she hurls the frog at the wall, rather than through her kiss, that the change takes place. So what would happen if the transformation was not as complete as it seemed? I imagined the birth of their first child as the moment when this came to light.

As I wrote, I found that I was drawing on my own experience of becoming a mother – my sense of bewilderment, and the contrast between my hopes and expectations, and the messy reality of birth and motherhood. From the moment he arrived, our son bore a very strong likeness to my husband. He looked nothing like me at all! I had the sudden realisation, as our baby was handed to me, that he was a stranger, and it would take time to get to know him. Nine months of pregnancy, antenatal classes and avid reading had not prepared me for the arrival of this new person who needed me for protection, love and food, right from his first breath.

The mother in my story, Ruby, is filled with all of these doubts and fears – will she be able to love this baby, this new stranger? Will she be the mother she had hoped she would be?

I also wanted to explore the moment when a couple becomes a family. For Ruby and Ricky the birth forces them to examine their relationship, as they begin their new roles as parents together.

The fairy tale allowed me to write about these themes in unexpected ways which I hope will raise a smile of recognition in other parents.

**CLAIR WRIGHT**

# About 'Bearskin and Bare-skin'

I've always loved stories about transformation – I've never been able to work out why werewolves are always presented as such horrors. I think being able to turn into a wolf and back would be a brilliant thing. And if you eat the neighbours, you could always get new ones. But invariably, being turned into an animal is regarded as a curse in most stories and someone has to go through hell to turn them back, or some great quest has to be completed and so on and so forth. We're so hell-bent on being human, despite the fact that most of us aren't terribly happy being human. Subconsciously, I suppose, as I didn't have a clear purpose in mind when writing the story, I wanted to turn the tables and have someone actively desire becoming an animal. There may be some shades of Angela Carter in there – she's one of the writers I admire immensely, and I love her animal/human tales in *The Bloody Chamber*.

The remainder of my inspiration came from a photograph I happened across in Marina Warner's *From the Beast to the Blonde: On Fairy Tales and their Tellers*. It shows a woman breastfeeding her (human) daughter and also a tiny bear cub. It originally appeared in *Wild Brother* (1921) by William Lyman Underwood, a story that told how an orphaned bear cub was taken in by a family and raised alongside their baby daughter (after Dad had shot the mother bear, naturally). The photograph certainly surprised me, if that's not too mild a term. There was a bit of shock on beholding it for the first time, and when I came to write my story I decided to use it as it was such an arresting image. The story of the girl who had a bear for a sister and wanted to turn into one came quite easily afterwards – I even named my protagonist 'Ursula' after the baby girl in *Wild Brother*.

The nuns were more-or-less deliberate – I noticed that in

numerous stories featuring feral children being "civilized", the task of humanizing them always falls to nuns! Just to be contrary I made the nuns kindly women who want the best for Ursula rather than the strict demagogues who usually turn up in these sorts of stories. Cerridwen I don't have a clue about, she just turned up!

**CARYS CROSSEN**

# About 'Crossing the Victoria Line'

When I was five or six, I received a magnificent Christmas gift from an aunt: an illustrated collection of Hans Christian Andersen fairy tales. I drove my parents demented for months requesting the stories over and over before bed. The detailed illustrations also fascinated me. Even today, they remain vivid in my memory. Thumbelina in a nutshell, the ugly duckling's transformation into a swan, the nightingale singing through an open window. However, the story and illustration that struck me most was 'The Little Match Girl'. The accompanying picture showed a blonde waif huddled in a doorway, a wooden box filled with matches in her lap. Dirty and wet, her large eyes peered out of the page and into my heart.

In London a couple of years ago close to Christmas, I waited for a shop to open and observed a young woman sleeping in the doorway. A clerk unlocked the double doors and gently spoke to the sleeping occupant. 'Madam, I'm afraid you'll have to move now.' He politely waited as she gathered her blankets and bags. Later, when I exited I noticed the same clerk across the road speaking with the woman where she had settled on a bench. He handed her a hot beverage and sandwich.

His simple act of kindness resonated with me, and the young woman harbouring in the shop doorway triggered memories of my fairy tale book from long ago. My precious childhood book is long lost. I reread 'The Little Match Girl' online and it spurred me to try adapting the story to a modern, London setting. Matches became a lighter, money is earned from singing, the grandmother changed to the much closer link with her mother. While her fate remains the same as in Hans Christian Andersen's original version from 1845, the stationmaster in my story came from the observation of a modern shop clerk's empathy.

**MARIE GETHINS**

# About 'The Salt Child'

'The Salt Child' falls, perhaps, into the 'forgotten' aspect of this anthology. I was first introduced to it by a storyteller friend, the lovely Zette Harbour, who had done a brief but spellbinding retelling on YouTube. I later found it, in an even briefer incarnation, in *Stories of the Spirit, Stories of the Heart*. Both times, I fell in love with the story.

I'm often drawn to stories which carry the theme of "letting go", perhaps because it can feel like the most terrible challenge we face, both in the everyday reality of endings in life and in the ultimate "letting go" of death. I revisit the theme over and over again in my own writing – I'm wondering, as I write this, if it's a preoccupation. Even my picture book, *Are You Sad, Little Bear?* explores death and dying with children. I was moved to write my picture books after having worked for years with young people who, for a multitude of reasons, felt themselves outsiders from the mainstream. And despite their differing circumstances, they often had something in common: large, philosophical questions about the meaning and purpose and pattern of their lives. Questions that religion or education hadn't answered for them. I felt that somehow, the stories that might have helped them had been lost.

Neither didactic nor moralistic nor religious, 'The Salt Child' belongs to that more ancient, earthy realm of folk tale which lives free of such constraints. It resonates deep within, and some half-forgotten ancient, earthy part of us hears and answers. In its simplicity, the story speaks of a letting go so profound that if we allow ourselves to do it, we may realise we are more than what we seem; that we are larger, wilder, more beautiful, more mysterious...

It takes us by the hand and brings us home.

**RACHEL RIVETT**

# About 'The Truth About Tea'

In October 2013 I attended a workshop run by Marina Warner at 'Wiv Words', the Wivenhoe literary festival which ran for two years. 'The Life of Stories' focussed on the interaction between teaching, reading, and writing fiction, with an emphasis on myths and fairy tales. We were instructed to bring something to the workshop which was precious to us. I brought a mother-of-pearl and copper ashtray, shaped like a bed warmer but small enough to fit in my hand, that a friend had given me twenty years earlier. Other people brought sensible things like jewellery so that, when Marina Warner gave us the story prompt, they could slot their little piece of memory into a storyline. I had the ashtray. A precious one, but still. I have yet to write a story about that ashtray, but it prompted some thoughts on old friends, parental guilt and tea.

The story I sketched out that day wove together several strands of ideas. Many years ago I had a friend who lived on Crucifix Lane, near London Bridge station. The first time she led me there, in the dark, under the railway bridges, always stuck with me. It was a setting that had been waiting for a story. The second idea was about character. I've always been interested in mothers and blame, particularly mothers in fairytales, wicked queens, who get criticised for "testing" all the so-called princesses who turn up, drenched on their doorsteps. Everyone automatically sides with the young women, but I felt those older women knew about the world and how to spot a fake. The mother in my story is a guardian, standing at the gates. The final thread was tea. There can never be enough tea.

**SARAH ARMSTRONG**

# About 'Girl on a Pied Horse'

I never intended to submit this story. I had two others I had been working on for months, and this one didn't even exist until the very last minute. Two nights before the submission deadline I had a dream about a girl galloping through the night on a black and white horse and I couldn't get it out of my mind. Who was that girl? Why was she fleeing through the night? The next day the answers presented themselves to me as I ate my lunch and I gave up all hope of doing anything else for the rest of the day. This girl was not going to let me rest until her story was written. It took me an hour. When it was finished I put it aside and tried to forget about it. There was no way this story could possibly be better than the two I'd been working on for months. The girl and her horse knew better, and would not stop galloping through my head, insisting that they belonged in this book. Eventually I gave in, edited things up and submitted them. As it turns out, they were right.

**SARAH HINDMARSH**

# Index
## of Writers with Biographies

**Sarah Armstrong** (p. 135)

Sarah Armstrong has published two novels with Sandstone Press, *The Insect Rosary* and *The Devil in the Snow*. Her short stories have been published in print and online, most recently by *For Books' Sake*. She believes that writing groups are an essential reminder that writing is fun, and is a member of Colchester Writenight. She teaches undergraduate and postgraduate creative writing for the Open University, and lives in Essex with her husband and four children.

**Carys Crossen** (p. 113)

Carys Crossen has been reading voraciously since ever she can remember and began writing stories at age nine. She studied literature at university and spent most of her time examining the werewolf and other monsters in popular culture. She currently works for the Civil Service while trying to become a writer/librarian/proper academic. She has published several non-fiction articles and some reviews of academic books, but 'Bearskin and Bare-skin' is her first published work of fiction. She lives in Manchester with her husband and an ever-growing book collection.

**Moira Garland** (p. 93)

Moira Garland lives in Yorkshire, and is retired from lecturing in college and adult education. She has an MA in Women's Studies and has raised a son alone. Her poetry has won competitions, and has also appeared in *The North*. Her short stories are published online at www.commuterlit.com and in print in *The Ham #1*. In the 60s she took up socialist-feminist activism, now confined to online involvement, but which informs much of her writing. When not writing she plays melodeon for Persephone Women's Morris, watches birds, gardens, and re-watches *Cabaret* – her all-time favourite film. Find her at: www.wordswords-moirag.blogspot.co.uk

**Marie Gethins** (p. 125)
Marie Gethins' work has featured in *The Irish Times*, 2014/15/16 National Flash Fiction Day Anthologies, *Flash: The International Short-Short Story Magazine*, *Litro*, *NANO*, *The Lonely Crowd*, *Wales Arts Review*, *The Incubator*, *Circa*, *Words with JAM*, *Firewords Quarterly*, *Word Bohemia* and others. She won or placed in The Short Story, Tethered by Letters flash, Flash500, Dromineer Literary Festival, The New Writer Microfiction, Prick of the Spindle and 99fiction.net. Other pieces have been listed in The London Magazine, Boulevard Emerging Writers, Bath Short Story Award, Bristol Short Story Prize, Brighton Prize, Fish Short Story/Flash/Memoir, James Plunkett Award, Listowel Writers Week Originals, Inktears, RTE/Penguin, Molotov Cocktail, Lightship, Doris Gooderson, Over the Edge and WOW! Award competitions. Marie is a Pushcart, Best of the Short Fictions, British Screenwriters Award Nominee and a recipient of the 2016 Frank O'Connor Bursary mentorship under Zsuzsi Gartner. She has a Master of Studies in Creative Writing from the University of Oxford and lives with her family in Cork, Ireland.

**Sarah Hindmarsh** (p. 143)
Sarah Hindmarsh is a private tutor by trade, and tries to be a writer in most of her spare time. She has self-published the award-winning *Animal Adventures* series for six to nine-year-

olds and the ever-popular *1001 Writing Prompts* series. She also has a growing collection of short stories and poetry published in various literary journals, magazines and anthologies. In her remaining spare time she walks her miniature poodle, Kohla, and competes in showjumping and dressage (with significantly more success in the showjumping) on her horse, Callie. Sarah can be found on Facebook and Twitter and blogs on various subjects, including issues surrounding literacy in young people at: http://creatingwithkohla.com.

**Angi Holden** (p. 35)
Angi Holden is a freelance writer and teacher, whose work includes prize-winning adult and children's poetry, short stories and flash fictions, published in online and print anthologies. She brings a wide range of personal experience to her writing, alongside a passion for lifelong learning, and has recently completed a Creative Writing doctorate. She was the winner of the inaugural Mother's Milk Books Pamphlet Prize and her pamphlet *Spools of Thread* will be published in 2017.

**Elizabeth Hopkinson** (p. 61)
Elizabeth Hopkinson is a fantasy writer from Bradford, West Yorkshire – home of the Brontë sisters and the Cottingley Fairies. Over 60 of her short stories and fairy tales have appeared in anthologies and magazines, and she is the winner of a number of awards. Her story 'Desperately Seeking Hephaestion' was a winner in last year's Liars' League/National Gallery competition, and can be listened to on YouTube. Elizabeth loves fairy tale and history, especially the 18th century, and is currently writing a trilogy set in a fantasy version of baroque Italy. Find her at: elizabethhopkinson.uk

**Dan Micklethwaite** (p. 17)

Dan Micklethwaite is a freelance writer and novelist based in West Yorkshire. He won the *Words with Jam* Short Story Competition 2016, and his other recent short fiction has appeared in *Unsung Stories, Gallery of Curiosities, BLÆkk*, and Flame Tree Publishing's *Swords & Steam* anthology. His debut novel, *The Less than Perfect Legend of Donna Creosote*, was published by Bluemoose Books in 2016, and shortlisted for the *Guardian*'s Not the Booker Prize. For more information (and for occasional pictures of the inside of his shed), you can follow him on Twitter @Dan_M_writer.

**Poppy O'Neill** (p. 11)

Poppy O'Neill's short stories have been published in *Halo* Literary Magazine, the National Flash Fiction Day Anthology 2016, A Room Of Our Own anthology and The Dangerous Women Project. Her non-fiction has appeared in *Oh Comely*, Sheroes of History, *Aesthetica* and *The Mother* magazine. She lives in Sussex with her husband and two children, and is currently writing her first novel and studying for an MA in creative writing at the University of Chichester.

**Ness Owen** (p. 101)

Ness Owen lives on Ynys Môn off the North Wales coast with her husband and three nearly-all-grown-up children. She writes stories, poetry and plays in between lecturing and farming. Her work has appeared in anthologies and journals including *Poetry Wales, Red Poets, Ink, Sweat & Tears, The Fat Damsel*, Arachne Press and Three Drops Press. Her short plays have been performed in a variety of venues including Clwyd Theatr Cymru, Sherman Cymru and Chapter Arts Centre, Cardiff. She is a member of Cybi Poets and can be found tweeting folklore and poetry (amongst other musings) @ness_owen

**NJ Ramsden** (p. 75)

Nathan 'NJ' Ramsden writes mostly short fiction, though he has become increasingly interested in translating medieval poetry. Influences include Donald Barthelme, H. P. Lovecraft, J. L. Borges, Angela Carter, classical mythology, and folktale.

He has published one novel (*Nothing's Oblong*), and has several short stories in print and online. He taught Creative Writing for several years. In his spare time he enjoys baking, learning Icelandic, and making music with synthesizers he builds himself.

He can be found online at: njramsden.wordpress.com

**Ronne Randall** (p. 39)

Ronne Randall was born in New York in 1947 and has lived in the UK since 1985. She has worked in book publishing since the late 1960s, and in 1980 began editing and writing mass-market and educational children's books – she has published more than 150 titles. She has a lifelong interest in traditional tales, rhymes and ballads, which led her, a decade ago, to do an MA in Folklore and Cultural Tradition at the University of Sheffield. Though still writing for children, she is now broadening her audience, and her stories have appeared in *Mslexia*, *The Forgotten and the Fantastical 2*, and *Words and Women 4* (Unthank Books). Married, with a grown-up son, Ronne lives with her husband and cat in Nottinghamshire.

**Rachel Rivett** (p. 131)

Author of three picture books, and shortlisted for SCBWI's Undiscovered Voices 2014 with her YA mythic fantasy, *Traitor Girl*, Rachel Rivett has an MA in Writing for Children from Winchester University. She is an aspiring Young Adult author with a love of mythic and dystopian novels; although, as someone famously pointed out, dystopian novels are ever

189

harder to write these days as governments steal all the best ideas for policy making. She and her husband have home-educated their four children, believing the best learning happens when people follow their hearts.

### Sophie Sellars (p. 51)

Born and raised in Suffolk, Sophie Sellars travelled the world as a Production Co-ordinator on major feature films before turning to writing. Her stories have been published in the *Telegraph*, the *Guardian* and *Shooter Literary Magazine* and she was the overall winner of the Daily Telegraph Travel Writing Prize for 2013. Her first stage play, 'The Drop Zone', was produced at the Southwark Playhouse in London in January 2017. She lives in Hertfordshire and can be found on Twitter as @ScribblingSoph

### Claire Stephenson (p. 71)

Claire Stephenson is a person-centred counsellor working with young people in West Yorkshire. She is one of the organisers of Fictions of Every Kind, a non-profit literary social event. Her solo work has appeared in various anthologies and collaboratively in the illustrated *Stories From The Forests of Leeds*. She lives in a housing co-operative with a six-year-old crystal enthusiast.

### Lynden Wade (p. 25)

Lynden Wade was home-schooled in a village in West Africa, giving her lots of time to read. The bright colours of illustrations to fairy tales, legends and medieval history – worlds away from the dry grasslands and termite hills around her – inspired her to write her own stories. Her muses include Joan Aiken and Rosemary Sutcliff. She is working on three historical novels, and has published a poem in one anthology and a fairy tale in another, *From the Stories of Old*. She loves tea shops, period drama, castles and trees. You can find her on: lyndenwadeauthor.weebly.com

**Clair Wright** (p. 107)
As an MA Literature student, Clair Wright spent a lot of time writing about other people's writing. Since becoming a mother she has got around to writing something of her own. She is a member of a creative writing group, the Yorkshire Writers' Lunch, with whom she finds creative support and encouragement. The group blog collectively (on a weekly basis) as: yorkshirewriterslunch.blogspot.co.uk and in 2015 they published an anthology entitled *Dining on Words*. Clair enjoys writing short stories and poetry. She has previously been published in the *Guardian* as Louise Wright, and in e-magazine *Kishboo*. Clair is married with two young sons.

**Mother's Milk Books**
is an independent press, founded and managed by
at-home mother Dr Teika Bellamy.

The aim of the press is to celebrate femininity
and empathy through images and words,
with a view to normalizing breastfeeding.
The annual Mother's Milk Books Writing Prize,
which welcomes poetry and prose
from both adults and children,
runs from September to the end of January.
Mother's Milk Books also produces and sells art
and poetry prints, as well as greetings cards.
For more information about the press,
and to make purchases from the online store,
please visit: www.mothersmilkbooks.com